Eternal Curse on the Reader of These Pages

Eternal Curse on the Reader of These Pages

Manuel Puig

University of
Minnesota Press Minneapolis

Originally published in Spanish as *Maldición eterna a quien lea estas páginas* by Editorial Seix Barral, S.A., Barcelona, in 1980. First published in the English language by Random House, Inc. First University of Minnesota Press edition, 1999. Reprinted by arrangement with Random House, Inc.

Published by the University of Minnesota Press
111 Third Avenue South, Suite 290
Minneapolis, MN 55401-2520
http://www.upress.umn.edu

Library of Congress Cataloging-in-Publication Data

Puig, Manuel.
Eternal curse on the reader of these pages / Manuel Puig.
p.   cm.
ISBN 0-8166-3536-6 (pbk.)
I. Title.
PR9300.9.P84E8   1999
813 — dc21
99-31003

Printed in the United States of America on acid-free paper

The University of Minnesota is an equal-opportunity educator and employer.

11 10 09 08 07 06 05 04 03 02 01 00 99   10 9 8 7 6 5 4 3 2 1

Part One

—What is this?

—Washington Square, Mr. Ramirez.

—I know "square" but not "Washington." Not really.

—Washington is the name of a man, the first President of the United States.

—Yes, I know. Thanks so much.

— . . .

—Washington . . .

—Forget it, it's not important, Mr. Ramirez. It's just a name and nothing more.

—Was he the owner of this land?

—No. They simply named it after him.

—"Named?"

—Yes. Why are you looking at me like that?

—Named . . .

—My name is Larry. Yours is Ramirez. And Washington is the name of this square, all right? The square is named Washington.

—I know. What I don't know is what one is supposed to feel when one says "Washington."

— . . .

—You said the name was not important. What, then, is important?

—Look, what's important to me doesn't have to be important to you. Different strokes for different folks . . . O.K.?

—But tell me what is really important.

—I'm paid to push your wheelchair, not give you my philosophy of life.

—You were hired by the agency, am I correct?

—Yes, and they told me to wheel you around and nothing else. The pay is lousy. And if I also have to give you English lessons, I want more money. The cost of living is high in New York, you know?

—Mister . . . Larry. I know English, I know the words. I know the words in French and in Italian. I know all the words in Spanish, my native language, but . . .

— . . .

—In my country I was very ill. I remember all the words, the names of things that can be seen, heard, smelled, tasted, touched. But other things that are . . .

— . . . in your head . . .

—No, no . . . though you'll see what I mean soon enough.

— . . .

—I know all the words.

—Really?

—Yes . . . Washington, Larry, square, young Larry, old Ramirez, very old, seventy-four, and trees, benches, grass, cement. But nervous breakdown, depression, euphoria . . . I don't know what these words mean. The doctors keep using them.

—Didn't they make themselves clear?

— . . .

—You should have asked.

—I know what the words signify. I've read their definitions in the dictionary. But maybe I haven't experienced them lately, so I understand them only up to a point . . .

—You really know all those languages?

—Yes. . . . What an ugly day.

—Is it too cold for you?

—No. Take me to the center of the square. . . . Last night, in a dream, we saw a tree like the one over there near the center.

—We?

—Yes. You and I and everyone. We saw it clearly.

—Which dream was it?

—The one last night.

—What are you trying to say?

—Every night we all dream. Sometimes we have more than one dream. Isn't that so?

—Yeah.

—And in last night's dream there was a tree like that one, and one of the branches bore a lot of fruit. But only that one branch.

—Look, Mr. Ramirez: people dream while sleeping. But each person's dream is a private affair.

—You mean you didn't see the tree last night . . . and the branch?

—No, I didn't.

— . . .

—No one else saw it. Only you. The only person in the whole world.

—Why?

—Because that's the way it is. When you dream you are completely alone.

—Don't go so fast. When the ride is bumpy it's bad for me, too rough.

—Sorry.

—The pain is starting up again.

—What pain?

—The one in my chest.

—Should we go back?

—It's getting very sharp . . .

—Listen, I'm going to take you back.

—No, not there, please . . .

—I don't want to get in trouble. If you don't feel well, let's go back.

—Please . . . don't go so fast.

—Sorry.

—Sorry? They say that all the time. What does it mean?

— . . .

—What does it mean?

— . . .

—Don't look at me like that . . . I know what sorry means. It means you shouldn't have done something. But what do you feel when you say it?

—. . .

—This pain is so sharp . . . please, Larry, say something, show me something in the street or here in the park, anything! . . . To make the pain go away . . . I can't stand it . . .

—You shouldn't have insisted on going out on such a cold day. It's your own fault.

—Take me into one of those houses. They are beautiful and old; they must be very cozy.

—They used to be homes; they're offices now. They belong to the university. We can't go in; people are working there, writing off lunches.

—That man . . . that one over there, what is he running away from? He doesn't look well.

—He's jogging. He's exercising.

—But his face, there's something wrong with him, he must be very sick.

—No, he's driving himself. It's good for him.

—But I thought that when people make faces like that they're suffering.

—Yes, he's straining. But it will make him feel better the rest of the day.

—How do you know?

—I jog, too. I run every morning, and maybe I have the same expression on my face.

—That woman crossing the street . . .

—What about her?

—Push me closer to her. The pain is so sharp, young man, you can't begin to imagine.

—. . .

—She brought her baby to the park, don't you see? . . . It's not wrong to come to the park in the cold . . .

—. . .

—And she brought her dog along, too.

—You're right.

—What's wrong with her teeth?

—What?

—Take me closer to her, please.

—Nothing is the matter with her teeth. She's smiling at the baby, that's all.

—Smiling?

—Yes. Let me guess, you don't know what that means either?

—No.

—Jesus.

—Smiling. Yes, of course . . . but what causes the upturning of the corners of her mouth and the brightening of her eyes?

—It's exhausting for me to explain every word to you. I won't.

—What do you mean you won't? . . . The pain is unbearable! Explain "smiling." Explain . . .

—When something pleases you, you smile.

—Plea . . . pleases?

—God, how can I? If you don't feel the pain in your chest; if you see the tree . . . your tree and the branch and all the fruit . . . and you want to eat a fruit, and you grab one and eat it, then maybe you'll smile.

— . . .

—Did you follow what I said?

—No, there were too many . . . words. But the pain has subsided.

—Sure, too many words. The importance of smiling? I know you don't understand, but a smile may mean nothing. One can smile and not feel a thing. People just do it. And I don't give a shit whether they do or don't.

—I dislike such language.

—Smiling is shit; it's false, it's empty most of the time.

—This is all much too confusing for me. That's why I want you to take me to the center of the square. I'll get a clearer perspective from there. I'll be at the same distance from all four corners, at least.

—It's much warmer today. The weather changes so quickly in this town.

—That's how it is.

— . . .

—We still have some time left. What street should we take?

—The same as always.

—Did you make that call?

—What call?

—The one to get me a raise.

—I called, but the secretary at the agency had already left for the day.

—You'll have to call again.

—Yes, I will.

—So, Mr. Ramirez, the same street then.

—The same one, please.

—There are others more interesting here in the Village.

—Have you taken notes on this neighborhood?

—Notes? I live here, and I've known the neighborhood since college.

—What are you saying?

—I studied at the university next to the square. I earned a degree.

—In what?

—History.

—Then why do you have this job?

—Is this an inquisition? Can't we talk about something else?

—I'd like to talk about the college you attended.

—Can't two guys have a conversation without getting into each other's business? Let's talk about sports or the news. Anything. Earthquakes, books . . .

—What is your favorite book?

—It's impossible to say. I've read so many books about so many subjects. Many have impressed me, but they can't be compared to each other. You can't expect an answer to such a question.

—When you go home, look through your library. Perhaps you'll find the book you like most.

—I don't have a library. I've moved so often that I had my books stored in the basement of a hardware store on Canal Street.

—Will you be staying at this place you have now for a long time?

—I hope so. If I can improve my financial situation a little.

—Do you have a large family to support?

—Yeah, one cat.

—So you live alone.

—Yes.

—Where? On which street?

—On Carmine, not far from here.

—I believe we crossed it once.

—Do you like chess, Mr. Ramirez?

—No.

—Do you play cards?

—No.

—Don't tell me you read horoscopes.

—I don't know.

—If there's something I can't stand, it's people who try to figure out their lives with horoscopes.

—I saw one of the nurses at the home studying a book on signs, and she told me that she and I could be friends because hers was also an earth sign—she was a Virgo.

— . . .

—I'm a Capricorn.

—That's quite a feat.

—And you?

—Several years ago I worked in an office, and the dumbest people, especially the younger women, consulted horoscopes to explain to themselves why nothing good had happened to them and why something good would happen. Most were trapped by external circumstances and by their own inhibitions.

—External circumstances?

—Yeah, jobs, money . . .

—And you wrote all that down and you can return to it and read it whenever you want.

—What?

—Maybe you reread your notes this morning and that's why you're talking about all of this now.

—I don't know what you're talking about.

—I wish I could check my notes so as to discuss them, too; that is, with someone eager to listen, of course.

—I haven't written anything down. I just remember.

—I remember things, too. I can remember everything I read now at the home. I have a good memory.

—I still don't understand. Those women were unimportant to me; I just remembered what happened.

—I remember all that I've read since I arrived in New York last week.

—Since you read so much, don't miss next year's predictions. The book containing them has just been published. It makes a good holiday present.

—The tone of your voice means you're mocking me, doesn't it?

—You're making progress. . . . By the way, Mr. Ramirez, that piece of paper lying on your table with my name on it and an arrow pointing to the word "nurse"—what was it?

—Nothing.

—Nothing? Look, I'll ask you again, and if you don't answer me, I'll . . .

—It had no significance, Larry.

—You're keeping something from me for some reason.

—It's nothing. A nurse asked me about you.

—The Virgo?

—No! The Virgo is young and pretty.

—Then which one?

—An older one. Yes. Old and ugly.

—What did she want to know?

—She and another even older asked who you were.

—And?

—It seems that they are attracted to just about any young man. They thought you were good looking and virile.

—How nice! Don't tell them anything. . . . What else did they say?

—Do you leave your cat alone all day long?

—What else did they say?

—Nothing. Well . . . one of the old nurses, not the Virgo, told me something. It seems she lives in the neighborhood and has seen you before.

—That's possible. What else did she say?

—Nothing.

—Come on, it's obvious you're not telling me everything.

—She said she's noticed you for a long time. And she always tells herself, "What a good-looking man, and he's always by himself. His hair's already turning gray. What's keeping him from finding himself a woman?"

— . . .

—And she wondered whether you had a job because she used to see you in the park, early afternoons, watching the old men play chess.

—I've been unemployed.

—Have you taken care of old people like me before?

—No, this is the first time.

—Why don't you get a better job?

—You're getting personal again. Let's talk about the world, reality, which is more important. Aren't you interested in relations between Egypt and Israel?

—I'm having trouble breathing today . . . something's wrong with me.

— . . .

—Now that I think about it, maybe I have taken notes all my life, but when I arrived here I had very little luggage with me.

—You've lost me again, Mr. Ramirez.

—I mean to say that I'm a person who likes to take notes. I take notes all the time at the home. And in the past, I suppose.

—I guess.

—But you don't?

—No, not really.

—How is that possible? Do you still remember things that happened long ago?

—Yes.

—Can everyone else or just you?

—Some people can.

—Not I.

—Maybe you're better off this way, Mr. Ramirez.

—Don't ever hide anything from me again.

—What?

—Don't you or anyone else dare . . .

—What right do you think you have to talk to me in that tone? Have you lost your mind?

—The doctor is going to be sorry! He's made me sound like an imbecile.

— . . .

—I looked in the encyclopedia for an explanation of memory. It was thorough, but I thought that memory applied only to recent events.

— . . .

—The nurse at the home pushes my wheelchair better than you do. The male nurse. Of course, the girls have an even gentler touch.

— . . .

—Why are you rummaging through the garbage? It's filthy.

—It isn't, Mr. Ramirez. Once in a while people throw away newspapers and magazines. I like magazines, but they're expensive.

—Don't start reading now. Pay attention to where you're going.

—I know what I'm doing.

—Carmine Street! You must live around here.

— . . .

—I've never been in a real home in this country.

— . . .

—Why don't you invite me to your place for a while? Is it far from here?

—It's close by. This street is only two blocks long.

—Good . . . no, don't turn; why are you turning?

—This street is ugly, and my apartment even more so.

—Is that true?

—I've only two small rooms.

—At the home I have only one. I'd like to see the interior of an American house.

— . . .

—Won't you invite me?

—No!

—Two small rooms, but cozy, I'm sure. There's no reason not to invite me.

—Two small rooms. The stove is in one, and is covered with grease, stalactites of grease and dust. Everything sticks to it. And there's no furniture, only a broken chair I found in the street. And on the floor, newspaper shreds that drifted in from God knows where. There's a mattress on the floor and a sheet that used to be white, but has turned to brown. And roaches galore.

—You don't have a blanket?

—No, I'm never cold. Sometimes it gets so warm that I have to turn off the heat. And I sleep without a pillow; it's healthier that way. You can see the filth in the apartment from the street or the neighbor's window.

—You're lying. These are all excuses for not inviting me. You're always impeccably clean. And what's more, if you don't want anyone to see your apartment, why do you allow people to look through the window?

—I don't have curtains.

—Don't start with that magazine again. Pay attention to where you're going.

—Don't worry. I know where I'm going. Back to your place. Time is up.

—You . . . here . . . at this hour?

—First, good evening, Mr. Ramirez.

—Are you here to take care of somebody else?

—No.

—Then . . .

—I hope you don't mind my coming without permission.

—Did the night watchmen let you in?

—They didn't see me, I'm sure.

—How did you open my door? I always lock it from inside.

—I may have come through the window. You'll never know.

—I'm imagining your visit, perhaps?

—Maybe.

—No, I'd rather that your visit be real.

—As you wish . . .

—Well, then, you are here. I'm not imagining you.

—It isn't too late for me to be here, is it? I know dinner is served at seven, but you never told me what time you go to sleep.

—I don't like your tone, Larry. It's too obsequious, too unctuous.

—I'm sorry.

—You're apologizing because your tone was hypocritical, wasn't it?

—It was, and I apologize.

—As you know, I still don't know what to make of certain tones. The expression of sincere regret . . . I wouldn't be able to recognize it.

—Maybe you'll recognize this . . .

—Get off your knees! . . . Others may be watching . . . these people are senile, but malicious.

—But the door is shut.

—They'll say you're servile; they won't understand. As for me, I appreciate a good penitent.

—Thank you. You're very generous.

—What are you doing here? It's almost midnight. I guess you must have your reasons for coming as a ghost, an hallucination.

— . . .

— . . .

—If I'm just an hallucination, it shouldn't matter if I bow my head.

—Your visit is real. If it weren't, it would mean . . .

—It wouldn't mean anything at all. I've made a financial miscalculation, and I don't have any money for dinner.

—Ah . . .

—I'm very hungry. I thought I could go to sleep without eating . . . but my stomach is beginning to growl.

—Are you in pain? Where do you feel pain?

—Right below my sternum.

—Is it a pang or merely a discomfort?

—It isn't very sharp yet.

—As you can tell, I'm not amused.

—I don't follow you . . .

—You were amused when I told you about my pain, the awful oppression, the terrible pangs in my chest. Now I'm not laughing at you.

—I don't know, Mr. Ramirez . . . maybe . . . it's possible that you aren't very good at reading other people's expressions. Maybe I was only trying to comfort you with a smile.

—Smiling is empty, false . . . shit, as you said.

—Mr. Ramirez, how's the food here?

—It's tasteless; but it's nutritious and plentiful.

—Do they give you enough?

—Yes. I always leave at least half on my plate.

—Where do they serve meals?

—In the big hall. But if I wanted to, I could eat in my room, providing I agreed to eat a little earlier.

—Mr. Ramirez. . . . What did we see some people taking to the park? I don't remember if both of us saw them . . . or was it only I . . . or you and then you told me about it?

—Some people take plastic containers filled with leftovers, which they give to cats or dogs, or bread soaked in milk, which they throw to pigeons.

—Ah . . .

— . . .

—I myself spend a lot of money on food, Mr. Ramirez.

—Yes, you burn up a lot of energy jogging, and you must replenish it.

—That's it . . .

—I don't like to eat very early, but I also don't like to eat in the dining hall with the rest of them. So I can gain by a sacrifice. If I eat in my room earlier, I will be spared having to look at their faces. And no one would know that I save more than half of my food in plastic containers . . .

—For my cat.

—Yes, I understood . . .

—Thanks . . .

—I've read that one can become teary-eyed often out of joy instead of pain. It seems that certain deep emotions, even when positive and pleasant, can make one cry.

—That's why you see me this way, Mr. Ramirez.

—Don't bow your head. I dislike that gesture.

—O.K., I'm going . . .

—If you weren't hungry, I'd ask you to stay and chat a bit.

—I can endure it, I assure you.

—No, just because you owe me a favor, it's not right for me to ask you to stay.

—There are many subjects I'd like to discuss with you, Mr. Ramirez.

—Nothing would flatter me more.

—Since you've been reading articles about this country's involvement in Vietnam, you must have asked yourself how those of us who were young at that time responded to what was happening, how we could drop napalm on innocent civilians . . .

—Did you fight in Vietnam?

—Yes, I participated in all the atrocities. I want to tell you all about it, but you must first tell me about yourself. The wiser man should begin.

—Me? . . .

—Yes, you must tell me everything.

—But Larry, don't you know that I . . . have forgotten . . . a lot?

—That could be one of your strategies for evading possible spies.

—I'm sorry, Larry, but suddenly I feel very tired. I must retire now.

—Then maybe some other day . . . I need your help, your advice . . .

—Again that mocking, scornful look . . .

—You still don't know how to read expressions.

— . . .

—Why are you silent, Mr. Ramirez?

— . . .

—I'm going.

— . . .

—But if you'd be so kind . . . the money for dinner.

— . . .

—You promised.

—Take what you need.

—Are you giving me your wallet?

—Excuse me, Larry . . . my pulse is getting so weak. I didn't drop it on purpose.

—Let me pick it up . . . I don't mind . . . stooping.

—I can see that.
—How much may I take?
—Whatever you need.
—Five . . . five bucks is enough. . . . Thanks.
—Don't mention it.
—Goodnight, Mr. Ramirez.

—It's raining. I should never have listened to you.

—It may stop soon, Larry.

— . . .

—Does my calling you Larry bother you? Or should I call you Mr. Larry?

—Larry's fine. But now we're stuck in the rain here on West Broadway. I told you it was going to rain. But you insisted on coming here.

—One of the nurses has repeatedly told me that I should see SoHo.

—The Virgo, I'll bet.

—Yes, that's very perceptive of you.

—Your horoscope must have been "pleasant outings in the rain."

—Now that I'm in SoHo I'm unable to see anything.

—Look at the nice puddles!

—I haven't talked about your raise yet.

—Yeah, what happened?

—I'm sorry, but most of the time someone's on the telephone at the home.

—In that case we'll stop at a bar and you can call from there.

—But I did talk to the nice secretary, finally.

—What did she say?

—She couldn't make the decision herself; she has to talk to the director of the foundation.

—She has to clear a two-dollar-a-day raise with the board of directors?

—That's what she said. What can I do?

—It's O.K., I don't mind going hungry.

—Ah, by the way, I forgot to give you something I brought for you.

—What is it?

—Food in hygienic plastic containers.

—Are you going to feed the pigeons?

—No, it's for you.

—For me?

—Don't look so offended . . . Larry.

—It looks disgusting.

—It's for your cat. I thought it would save you some time.

—No, thanks. I give my cat milk and canned food. That canned stuff stays good for two weeks.

—Oh, I didn't know.

—This food is awful. They'll kill all of you in the home. Food stinks in New York, that's why I'm very careful. I eat health foods whenever I can. Greens, fish, no grease or starch. No stimulants, no coffee or tea, sugar is the worst.

—Leave it there, Larry, or throw it in the basket when we reach the corner.

—Don't give me that look! Galleries are closed in the morning, I told you.

—I don't want to see paintings; I don't want to go inside places.

—Well, I can't wheel you around in the rain.

—If we could at least move to a place where I wouldn't have to look at these fire escapes . . .

—What's wrong with them?

—What a pointless question. Lately I haven't read anything on fire escapes, so there's nothing I can tell you about them. All I know is I'm not going to sit here and look at them any longer.

—Where the hell can we go?

—Please take me somewhere else.

—But it's pouring. We're lucky to find this awning.

—You work only a couple of hours three times a week, and we have to stand still like this.

— . . .

—I made a list of questions I wanted to ask you, but I left it at the home. I've been reading a lot and have some doubts about certain things.

—What have you been reading?

—The *Encyclopaedia Britannica* and history books. Do you remember how just a few days ago I didn't know much about Washington? Well, now I do. And I seem to remember everything I've read. I don't know for how long I will, though.

—What subject did you find most interesting?

—Argentina, my native country, is mainly inhabited by Spanish and Italian immigrants.

—That interests me.

— . . .

—Tell me more. I have an Italian grandfather, my father's father. His name was Giovanangelo.

—But your last name is John.

—When my grandfather disembarked, Immigration mangled his name.

—After you told me you'd been in Vietnam, I read all I could find about it.

—I was never in Nam.

—What do you mean? You said you had been drafted.

—I refused to go.

—Was it that easy to evade the draft?

—No. When they asked me why I resisted, I recited the history of colonialism and imperialism in Indochina.

—Did they listen to you?

—After my performance, they didn't want me, and kept rescheduling an appointment at six-month intervals until I was over the age limit. Others were braver. They enlisted and propagated mutiny . . .

—Sabotage . . . in the service?

—Yes.

—How many times did you make your speech about colonialism?

—Once was enough. After they heard it, they were only too delighted to find a legitimate reason to reject me. I was going to be twenty-six in about nine months. That was the cutoff age for the draft.

—I was convinced you had fought in Vietnam.

— . . .

—Why did you lie to me?

—We never discussed the subject, so don't be irritating. I'm on edge today.

—Why?

— . . .

—Don't look at him, please.

—Who?

—The man walking to the corner.

—Do you know him?

—Larry, please, don't let him come near me. Take me inside the store.

—The guy's gone. He turned left on Prince Street.

—Larry, I know you're not paid to listen to my troubles, but I assure you something bad may happen to me and I don't know how to prevent it.

—Bad in what sense?

—Don't go! Don't look! Come back! Please . . .

— . . .

—Larry!

—I just wanted to get a better look. He's just an ordinary guy. He entered an apartment building, a tenement.

— . . .

—Maybe he resembled somebody from your past. Somebody who harmed you. But he's gone now, soaking wet, too.

—Larry, please don't tell anyone about this. It's a secret.

—You'd better not tell me any more, then.

—But I don't want you to think that I'm imagining things. Unfortunately, time will prove me right.

—I believe you, Mr. Ramirez.

—I know you don't. But you'll see soon enough. That

man's been followed and he won't be able to escape, they've really got him this time.

—Who are "they"?

—We shouldn't be around because we won't be able to help. That's the problem.

— . . .

—If I could only bear this pain; you can't imagine how sharp it is.

—You're hurting again?

—Didn't you know?

—No, I didn't.

—That's right, you're not paid for that either. But it's as if somebody were tearing a piece of my chest out.

—I'm sorry it hurts so bad.

—And still you didn't realize it.

—How the hell was I supposed to know since you didn't say anything?

—I don't want to take advantage of you. After all, you're young, what can you know about any of this?

—I'm not that young, Mr. Ramirez. I'm thirty-six. Besides, I'm not inhuman.

—Thirty-six?

—Yes. Don't I look it? Some people think I'm even older.

—Then you must leave immediately. I'll ask the store owner to call the home. They'll send someone for me.

—Don't be ridiculous; I'll take you back. Being thirty-six doesn't mean one will be shot by gangsters. The real danger is in losing your hair.

—Don't joke; this is a terribly important matter.

—Who's joking? It's a crucial time in a man's life. Some men have to get hair transplants, wear wigs, comb their hair forward, dye their hair, wear beards, anything. In this country hair is a big deal.

—Please go now.

—O.K., Mr. Ramirez, now you are the one who should

stop joking. What is this bullshit anyhow? You don't believe all that stuff; why would anyone want to hurt me? Your fears are imaginary. You're no fool, you know they are. Besides, you have the whole day to brood. For two hours spare me the grief. Especially today.

—Pardon me. It's so hard for me to explain.

—Just remember you're not in your country, with all that turmoil. You're in New York. It's not that safe here, but who cares about you or me?

—Are you sure?

—Jesus, I already told you, I can't take any more of your paranoid questions.

—Larry, I'm sorry, I didn't mean anything I said about that man. It was all an act. I wanted to see how you would react, to see if you thought I was crazy and say yes to everything.

—What the hell . . . don't you trust me?

—How can I? I hardly know you.

—My only interest is to do this job with as little hassle as possible.

— . . .

— . . .

—I guess this morning you couldn't go jogging, what with the rain.

—It wasn't raining this morning.

—Do you exercise every day?

—Yes, every morning.

—Anything in addition to jogging?

—I swim, jump rope, do gymnastics. I go hiking, ride bicycles. Anything to relieve this terrible tension.

— . . .

—Why are you looking at me like that?

—Your hands are trembling, Larry.

—There are days I feel very nervous, that's all.

—Do you take drugs?

—I don't even drink coffee. I hate stimulants.

—What's the matter with you?

—Nothing. Let me have the shakes in peace.

— . . .

—The world is full of things and some people can't reach out for them.

—Why not? Are you referring to me?

— . . .

—Do you get up early?

—Yes, early, it's discipline. I do stretching exercises as soon as I get up. I warm up by running a few blocks, then I stop and let my pulse slow down. Then I run a few miles, down to Battery Park. And get a blast of sea air. After running I have breakfast; food never tastes better. If I could spend the whole day running, I'd be fine.

—Do you like mornings, or do they bore you?

—Before traffic gets heavy and noise begins, you feel fresh.

—But that's before morning starts. What about afterward?

—You have to plan the day, even when you're unemployed. It's hard to do. You have to fill a void . . . with chores and activities. Shopping, the laundry, lunch, a walk, looking through the want ads, dinner, television. It doesn't work . . . you don't feel expansive, enjoy things; you sleep more and more. . . . Days become shorter, tasks more burdensome; you do less and less.

—Larry, the rain is beginning to stop. You can take me back now.

—O.K., let's go.

—Not that way, please!

—Why not?

—It's a longer route, and I'm getting cold.

—No, it's a shortcut. We'll get back faster.

—Even if it's longer, the other way is better. There are fewer puddles.

—Nonsense, we won't land in any puddles.

—I beg you, let's not take any risks.

—What risks?

—I don't care about you, stubborn as you are; but as for me, I don't want to take any risks. Please stop! Not this way . . .

—Stop flailing about! I know what I'm doing.

—You can take all the risks you want, but don't expose me to danger, do you hear? Don't turn left!

—You're white as a sheet; what's the matter?

—Fool! Stop it, please stop! Turn back, will you!

—What's the matter? You're perspiring . . .

—Through which door did he disappear?

—Who?

—The man. The man who was following us.

—I thought you said that you had lied and were testing me.

—Have we passed the door already?

—Yes. It's where those kids are playing.

—I didn't see any kids.

—Turn around, they're still there.

—You're trying to confuse me.

—Don't be afraid, we're perfectly safe.

—Now please go faster; it would be worse to turn back.

—You shouldn't be sweating in such cold weather.

—Please go faster. But I don't want you ever to come back. I don't want to be responsible for what may happen to you.

—What? Are you firing me?

—It's better this way, believe me.

—Jesus, now you're screwing me. I need the job.

—Don't worry, I'll see to it that you're paid for the whole week.

—It's nice to be outside in this kind of weather.

—Two days of steady rain were enough. I don't know what I would have done if it hadn't cleared up today.

—It sure is clear.

—Larry, your face looks different today. Is it because of the weather?

—No, I'm pleased about the raise.

—The truth is that the secretary hasn't called me back yet.

—Then how come I got the raise?

—I get an allowance for books, and I decided that your raise was more important . . . for my health.

—That's nice of you, Mr. Ramirez, I appreciate it.

—I still have books that I haven't read at the home.

—Listen, we can go to the library and borrow books.

—But I'm not a citizen. I don't have a card.

—You can use mine. But I think it's possible simply to go in, give them your address and have them send you a card.

—Wonderful.

—Would you like to go now?

—No, it's very nice sitting out here.

—I enjoy it, too.

—It's unusually warm for December.

—Strange that you're not very restless today.

—I'm enjoying the sun.

—The second day we went out it was sunny and you didn't want to stop for a second.

—It's good to rest awhile.

—Do you get much sun in the garden of the nursing home?

—Yes.

—That's nice.

—Larry, since we're sitting here so peacefully, let's discuss a few matters.

—Sure, what would you like to talk about?

—Well, it just occurred to me that I'm twice your age. So you could very easily have been my son.

—True.

—Well, how can I put it? You see, I would like to know what fathers and sons talk about. I'm not sure, I may have had a son. But I've already told you about the trouble with my notes.

—So?

—Well, maybe if you talked to me as a son I would know what to ask as a father.

—But fathers are supposed to have answers; sons are the ones with questions.

—Fathers have answers . . .

—Well, they always know everything and give orders.

—I couldn't talk to you like a father, then.

—I guess not.

—But I want to know what fathers and sons talk about when they are by themselves.

—Now I realize why you wanted me to sit. It was a trap.

—I want to find out certain things, that's all.

—Go to a few movies instead, or watch some TV.

—No, those stories are made up, I don't trust them.

—You might find them entertaining.

—Fathers give answers, you say; are they good, thoughtful answers, or ready-made, synthetic ones like my doctor's?

— . . .

—I have an idea. Talk to me like a father and teach me. I will listen as if I were your son.

—That's not as easy as you think.

—Repeat what your father says to you.

—I haven't seen him in five years.

—Does he live far from New York?

— . . .

—It doesn't matter. Just repeat what he said to you years ago. That should be easy since you remember everything so well.

—Well, he didn't say much. He wasn't around much.

—When did you usually see him?

—At night. Sometimes at night, and for a few hours on weekends.

—Were you alone with him during those hours?

—No, I remember being alone with him only on two occasions.

—Who else was usually there?

—My mother, my brother and my sister.

—Do they all live far from here?

— . . .

—Have you gone a long time without seeing them?

— . . .

—And both times you were alone with him, what did he say?

—I don't remember exactly what he told me.

—Did he order you around?

—No, I just remember being with him and enjoying it.

—Say anything to me that he might have said.

—Well, once we were on a lawn near the parkway, flying a kite. It was early Sunday morning and we were alone. He must have shown me how to fly it.

—Did he?

—Yes, I guess he did. But that wasn't so important. It was being with him that mattered.

—Father, teach me how to fly a kite.

—I'm not your father.

—Help me. Proceed. I want to hear what he said.

—I told you, I don't remember.

—Please try.

—It's impossible.

—You don't want to tell me.

—I don't remember.

—What about the other time you were alone with him?

—We were playing catch in front of the house. It was our first time. Our first and only time. I remember how poorly he threw the ball, how clumsy he was. And that my mother had a better arm.

—Then she was there; you were not alone with your father.

—No, she wasn't there. But I remember making the comparison. My father didn't want to play too long. I kept begging him not to quit, to play some more. But he ignored me.

—Were you persistent?

—Yes.

—What words did you use?

—I don't remember.

—You don't want to tell me. Even if this horrible pain were to kill me, you wouldn't.

—What pain?

—You know very well.

—What about me? It's no fun to recollect and talk about all this crap.

—It isn't crap. You said you enjoyed being with your father that day.

—True.

—What did you enjoy so much?

—Spending time with him. I used to spend so much time with my mother.

—What was the difference?

—I was very attached to her. I just needed to spend time with my father, that's all.

—Doing what?

—That's really none of your business.

—It's not that I want to find out anything about your

personal life. What I want to know is what a father says to a son. Why don't you try to recall someone else's father? Somebody you liked or didn't like; it's all the same to me.

—I remember him being nasty and brutal. He would be silent and not complain about things. Then all of a sudden he would explode and hit me or my sister or my brother. I don't remember his exact words at those times; they were more like grunts.

—What did you kids do to make him so angry?

—Played, fooled around, got into mischief.

—How hard would he hit you?

—Very hard. I once heard him sawing off a piece of a two-by-four in the basement. Making a nice club to hit me with. He was a good carpenter. I was sitting upstairs, defiant, waiting for him to come up and get me, reading a magazine.

—Did he come up?

—Yes, he beat me with relish. It hurt terribly, and I howled. The beating seemed to last a long time; but I knew I would survive and that, strong as he was, he couldn't break me, even with that plank.

—Was he somebody you didn't like? The father of a friend?

—No, my own.

—First you talked about a man you enjoyed being with, who may have taught you to fly a kite. Now you talk about a vicious man, trying to baffle me by saying they are one and the same.

—Listen, I'd be glad to stop talking about this.

—Not now that you have completely succeeded in confusing me. It's impossible that you would want to spend time with someone who beat you.

—Anything you say.

— . . .

—He had a gentle, easy side, and a blind, violent one. I

think it's because he so often gave in to my mother.

—I'm not sure my interpretation is correct. Mainly I have this impression that if you love something you don't want to break it. And if you hate it, you do. Am I right?

—Yes, but it gets more involved.

—If you don't mind, tell me how you felt when you loved your father.

—As a matter of fact, I do mind. What happened to your chest pain?

—It's gone. Why? Would you rather see me in pain?

— . . .

—Maybe you wouldn't mind telling me how you felt when you hated him.

—I wanted to kill him.

—With your hands? A gun? A club? Or would you have liked to see him struck down by lightning?

—I'm not sure.

—Maybe lightning, Larry.

— . . .

—Father, I have a very strong chest pain.

—Cut that "father" shit out.

—I wasn't looking at you, I was looking at that beautiful old tree. Why would I want to call you Father?

— . . .

—Father, I've lost all my notes and I need them. I know I will never recover them, but I still miss them.

—Gee, can you hear the tree talking to you from all the way over here?

—I'm getting no reply, unfortunately.

—May I suggest we go back?

—You should have picked one with fewer steps, Larry.
—They all have steps.
—None with more than this one, I'm sure.
—Stop griping.
—For me, the way up was smooth. But you went through a lot of trouble.
—Let's get you registered for a card.
—They don't look friendly, these people.
—Librarians all look like that.
—They are very busy now; they won't take care of us.
—Don't worry about it.
—Stop pushing, let's stay here.
—Nonsense, we have to get you registered. They won't bite.
—What are those magazines over there?
—They're from all over the world. Do you want to look at them?
—No. Show me books.
—The whole place is full of books.
—The ones you would like to show to me.
—We could check the Astrology section.
—Why?
—It may interest you.
—I don't think so. What's more, I thought you disliked all that.
—We're here to satisfy your curiosity, not mine.
—Find something that both of us will be interested in. I don't like it when you complain.
—Who's complaining?
—Point to the books you would be delighted to show to me.
—Well, all right. There's a small selection of books on Marxism.

—. . .

—In the second aisle. They have a few things here. Volume One of *Capital;* all libraries have Volume One.

—Why's that?

—A minor condescension to the subject. They don't expect anyone to read or study all three volumes. So they just throw the first one in. Like the Gideon Bible in motels.

—The name Marx has come up so frequently that I looked it up in the encyclopedia. I remember the face, chubby with a big gray beard.

—That's him.

—What makes *Capital* one of your favorite books?

—Well, it's not a favorite in the sense that *Wuthering Heights* would be for someone.

—Is *Wuthering Heights* also one of your favorite books?

—No. Actually, I never read it.

—I did; it's in the library at the home. I read it in two days. This past weekend. Why haven't you?

—I don't know.

—When I read it I imagined that the nurse, the Virgo, was reading it to me. Reading it aloud. Well, come to think of it, she did start reading it to me. I asked her to; just one page. Because the author is a woman; did you know that?

—Someday perhaps you'll introduce me to this nurse.

—She won't like you.

—Why not?

—Honestly, I can't give you a reason. Maybe I'm wrong, but she's too different from you.

—I'm glad you've found somebody you like, Mr. Ramirez.

—But it's no use. She's always busy on the job; she never has time for me. And then . . .

—Then what?

—Nothing.

—You were going to say something.

—When she goes home she's even busier. Not like you or me. She has a daughter and a husband to look after. But I asked you if you knew that *Wuthering Heights* was written by a woman.

—Yes, I know.

—When you read it, who will you imagine is reading it to you?

—I never thought of it that way. I love to read, love words and phrases. There's nothing better than spending a few hours with a good book. It gives me great pleasure; I never imagined someone reading to me.

—Larry, when I read a book written by a man, I hear a young man's voice.

—It doesn't make any difference to me who writes the book. But perhaps we should find you some novels by women. You seem to miss them . . .

—She's not going to have time, I told you. A page at most. Now, Larry, tell me, when you read a book by a man you admire, such as Marx, I guess, whose voice do you hear?

—I guess my own.

—But you're not sure.

—No, I'm not sure, Mr. Ramirez.

—And when you talk to yourself, is it your voice you hear?

—Hmmm. I don't think so.

—Then whose?

—I don't know.

—Please concentrate.

—When you talk to yourself, one part always sees and judges what the other is doing. Like when you're trying to make a decision.

—You hear two voices, then. One is yours, but the other one? Whose is it?

—Sometimes one part gets vicious.

— . . .

—Studying the floor, Mr. Ramirez? What's so fascinating about it?

—Eh? . . .

—Why are you looking at the floor?

—I hear only one voice. Even when two parts of me talk to each other. But it is not my voice. . . . It's a young voice. It's a voice that sounds well; it's strong, determined, and its tone is pleasant. Like an actor's voice. But when I have to call a nurse or anybody, I hear my real voice. It's raspy, quavering, and I don't like it.

—At a certain age you have to expect that.

—If I could only stop hearing the young voice . . . maybe then I would get used to mine.

—Look, you said you wanted to know what books I enjoy. Here's *State and Revolution,* one of my favorites. It is really a remarkable work.

—By whom?

—Lenin.

—I like his face. There's a big picture of him in a glass case in the Kremlin now. I saw it in the encyclopedia. It reminded me of somebody. Of course, I don't remember who.

—It's a very readable book.

—I would probably need my notes to understand it.

—If you understand horoscopes you will understand this.

—Who told you I read horoscopes? That's very peculiar of you. You despise astrology and yet you want to believe that I like it. Which means you feel better if I'm a fool. You want me to be a fool. At the same time, you have to spend time with me. So it is very strange of you, young man, isn't it? You prefer to think that you're spending time with a fool, that you are degrading yourself. Do you feel better when you degrade yourself?

—Don't know, I have to think about that.

— . . .

— . . .

—*Capital* and *State and Revolution.* I think I understand your preferences. Aren't you afraid to show them?

—No, you can talk about anything in this country. Just don't act on your beliefs. You can read whatever you like.

—Would it frighten you to act?

—No, I don't think so. Sometimes I'd like the opportunity.

—To do what?

—Maybe get involved in union activities.

—Are they illegal here? What would be frightening about them?

—No, they're not illegal, but a Marxist has ways of struggling and goals that would bring him into conflict with union bureaucracy.

—Lower your voice.

—In addition to fighting bosses, you'd also have to go up against union leadership.

—This is much too complicated for me; better change the subject.

—Let me give you an example. Several years ago I worked for the civil service. One day the offices were closed because of a heavy snowstorm. We weren't paid for the day, and lost one vacation day to boot. It was the union representative who walked through the office the next day, informing us we'd been shafted. He made the announcement and left without talking to anyone, asking for opinions or telling us what the union was going to do. I looked around me and people seemed crushed. They had no outlet to vent their anger and frustration, so they turned against themselves. The rep should have called a meeting, asked the people for . . . strategies, suggested some of his own.

—What do you mean by "turned against themselves"?

—Something was taken from us, unjustly. There was outrage and anger and a desire to get it back. When these feelings are not discharged or channeled into action that remedies the situation, the individual feels helpless and re-gresses.

—The way you talk sounds familiar, but I'm not sure who you remind me of.

—Does it annoy you?

—What did you do that night?

—The solidarity that would have resulted from a meeting —the heightened consciousness—could have informed other struggles. Instead, the union rep came by three weeks later and told us of the steps the union would take to redress our grievances. By then people were so demoralized and withdrawn that they didn't expect the union to win. This is an example of a completely bureaucratic approach. Of the noninvolvement of the rank-and-file. Six months later the union actually won the case, and our vacation day was re-stored. But the next time a really major issue came up and the union had to organize its members to fight, it had to overcome apathy, cynicism, the effects of its own past mis-takes. So you see the difference between maintaining an administration and building a social movement.

—You do remember everything, so you must remember what happened that night you thought you'd lost a day's pay. Did you sleep?

—Of course. I was very frustrated at work and depressed and confused.

—Please use words that mean more to me. What you say doesn't tell me what was going on inside you.

— . . .

—Say something! Don't make me beg! Frustration, con-fusion: Where do you feel them?

— . . .

—Do you feel bodily pain?

—Yes. In my stomach and chest and throat. A constric-tion, Mr. Ramirez.

—How do you ease the pain?

—There's no formula.

—Tell me about your chest pains. What causes them?

—I feel like all my organs are clenched like a fist.

—The chest pains, please, what causes them?

—I don't know. Being with a woman I like, and desire . . .

—Yes . . .

—That's the main cause.

—But if you like her, what's so painful about being close to her?

—I always think about my faults; that she won't like me because my nose is too big, my hair is falling out, my voice is harsh, or I'm not funny, or articulate . . . I always throw a monkey wrench in.

—What gives you a stomachache?

—Anxiety.

—Give me an example, please.

—I just gave you the one about the office. When you're attacked like that, even though it's unjust, there seem to be repercussions. One part of you rejects the accusation, another masochistically accepts it. These two impulses get tied up; you want to vomit the knot, discharge it. And I think there's good reason for this feeling. The masochistic part has to do with old identifications that have been internalized. Internalization is like swallowing something, eating something, incorporating something. Vomiting or spitting is the reverse process.

—You sound like my doctors. You have the same way of putting things. Not very personally.

—I learned a lot from that process; you can, too.

—What?

—Analysis.

—Are you seeing doctors, too?

—No, but I did several years ago. I can't afford it now. Shrinks are expensive.

—On what do you vomit?

—The floor, the street. Somebody else's desk or chair.

—Whose chair?

—Anything belonging to someone else.

—Anyone in particular?

—It doesn't matter as long as it's somebody else's property. The subway, the sidewalk, places where you're not supposed to spit, places with fixed rules.

—Promise you'll never vomit on my chair.

—O.K. Besides, it's powerful figures that you think of doing it to. Not helpless creatures like yourself.

—I'm sick, but that doesn't mean I'm helpless.

—You're pretty dependent. It seems like you want me to fill you with thoughts, ideas, feelings. Sometimes I feel like you're trying to suck life out of me.

—The encyclopedia could give me all the answers I get from you. But it can't push my wheelchair!

—I won't argue with you. I didn't know you could raise your voice like that. They might ask us to leave!

—The encyclopedia plus anybody, even a child, to push my chair, could replace you!

— . . .

—It's your fault if I spoke too loud.

—I don't think we disturbed anyone, Mr. Ramirez.

—Somebody could have heard what we were talking about.

—Now if you whisper like that, Mr. Ramirez, I can't hear you.

—Don't talk so loud, please.

—Now you blame me for the ruckus! . . . And who the hell cares what we're talking about?

—Don't you know that my troubles in my country had to do with that same madness? And I'm not sure that the authorities here would like any further complications. You're so irresponsible. Don't you realize I'm a foreigner, and I'm supposed to be grateful for the hospitality?

—You're not exactly a threat to the state in your wheel-chair, but sometime you must tell me about your politics.

—I never had anything to do with politics.

—How do you know? You may have forgotten that, among other things.

—Something inside tells me. I thoroughly despise politics.

—It matters a lot to me. We don't agree then.

—I'm glad we don't.

—But you came here through the auspices of that human rights committee; you never told me that. I found out anyway.

—I have an older brother in Argentina, my only relative. He's rich; he paid for my trip.

—Why does this committee take care of you?

—My brother has influence, I've been told; and he's asked them to help me. He pays well, too.

—It all sounds funny to me.

—Larry, why are you asking me all these questions?

— . . .

—I found out in the newspaper that the trouble in my country started with a leftist uprising. . . . Look, Larry, you don't know it, but you could be getting involved in something messy. Let's get out of this aisle. I don't want to be next to your favorite books.

—Thanks. The food agreed with my system.

—Thank you for paying, Mr. Ramirez.

—For a few dollars I assured myself of a nutritious meal. If it hadn't been for you I wouldn't have known about these bizarre diets.

—The menu was better day before yesterday, don't you think?

—No, I liked today's very much. We'll see about day after tomorrow's.

—Are you going to treat me each time I see you?

—I don't need my clothing allotment. I don't need any new clothes. I'd rather eat better food.

—I don't want to take advantage of you, I mean.

—The first snowfall of the season; does it have special significance in this country?

—None at all.

—It makes me feel like eating cake. Yesterday I read that somewhere in . . . well, I don't remember exactly where they bake something, something sweet on the first day it snows.

—Nothing like that here. People bitch.

—I'd give anything to eat something sweet; but it would be bad for me, Larry. Isn't this room squalid?

—Well, you have privacy, at least.

—I had a few posters up for a while, cheap ones that I could afford; but I quickly got tired of them. Because I spend so many hours, almost the whole day, in this tiny room, I don't like to go into their so-called recreation hall and see the other guests, the rest of the debris.

—You need a TV in this room.

—I had one, but told them to take it away. I'm arthritic; I don't want something similar to happen to my mind.

—I've noticed that the Virgo comes to your room quite often.

—She never comes when I'm alone; I always have to ring for her.

— . . .

—I noticed the way she looked at you.

—It's allowed, Mr. Ramirez.

—You were right about dreams. You couldn't have had the same one I had last night.

—Why?

—You were in the dream.

—I always am, in mine.

—I never . . . put that magazine down and pay attention to me! A few days ago I saw a face I liked very much in the encyclopedia. It was the face of Edith Cavell, an English nurse, a heroine of the First World War. She was captured in Belgium and shot by the Germans.

—I never heard of her.

—She was young; she was working in the trenches.

—Did she get trench mouth?

—What is that?

—It's an infection you get from kissing. You get pimples and scabs. When we were kids they used to say "Don't kiss Carol, or this one or that, or you'll get trench mouth." I don't know if the term is used anymore.

—You joke around because you haven't seen Edith Cavell's beautiful face. It's simply ignorance on your part, and I won't put up with it. But let me tell you my dream. I saw her being left behind by the English troops; she wouldn't leave the side of the wounded. Some of them were in critical condition; she hoped to save them. The bad thing was that she was sure that the Germans were not going to do anything to her. But this German general, a young one, that's you, came and asked her to make love to him. She refused, and he ordered her executed at dawn. I felt so impotent; I wanted to save her, to tell her to run, but I could find no way to make myself heard.

—Nice picture of me. And an interesting one of yourself.

—Tell me about your dream.

—I once had a dream about a hunchbacked tuna.

—I want you to tell me last night's dream.

—I don't remember it. You have to settle for the tuna.

—I'm listening.

—There was a green fish on the floor, lying on its side. It was a rather fat fish, and I had never seen anything like it before. There was someone else, a woman, in the room with me, and I asked her, what is that? And she said, "Oh, that's only a hunchbacked tuna," and I guess I was satisfied with her explanation.

—Who was the woman?

—I don't know. In the morning, I asked myself what the dream must have been about. The previous evening I had been with a woman; we made love and I remembered feeling the roundness of her back and shoulders. Also, the color of her rug was the green of the fish. I told myself, "My God, that's Debbie." Something must have disgusted and confused me that evening; it was resolved in the dream.

—I guess that wasn't that easy to figure out.

—Actually, I had a whole series of fish dreams. I once dreamt about a Nova Scotia mackerel. It was a large, bulky fish, cut in half; and I was about to slice off a thick steak for myself. The meat was red and raw, and I looked inside the fish. Again, there was a woman with me, who said, "That's a Nova Scotia mackerel," and that it would be all right to eat a piece.

—Go on.

—It was a strange dream, and in the morning I wondered what it signified. Several years ago, I took a vacation with a woman I lived with, and went to Nova Scotia. She was a big hearty woman, and although I had never seen a mackerel before, I imagined that, by the sound of its name, it was vigorous and powerfully built. She was the Nova Scotia mackerel, and I was given permission in the dream to have sex with her. I had to picture the woman as a fish, and sex as eating.

—Why?

—It's called repression.

—I'm sure you cared more for the second woman.

—Yes, I liked that mackerel.

—Who was she? I want to know.

—None of your business; she was just a woman I lived with.

—Your face changed when you talked about her; you seemed very pleased to remember her.

—What kind of expression did I make?

—It was not only in your face. Now that I think about it, I've never seen you change so drastically and suddenly.

—Change?

—I wish I could explain myself; you know I don't understand those things. Maybe if you tell me more about her. Who was she? I want to know.

—Hey, look, stop prying.

—Won't you tell me?

—No!

—She must have been important to you, wasn't she?

—Listen, Mr. Ramirez, why was that old couple in the lobby so nasty to us?

—I don't remember.

—Did something happen between you and them?

—I couldn't care less about them; they're people of no importance.

—But they were nasty to me, too; I'd like to know what happened.

—Nothing, really, the nurse had promised to read to me yesterday, but she had to look after that old hag since she made such a fuss about her cold.

—So?

—The Virgo nurse, you know, she's such a loving creature, she wanted to be with me, so she put the three of us together, and tried to read to us. Not what I wanted, just the newspaper. And the old hag, really her husband, started to make the most stupid remarks, and I laughed in his face. Wouldn't you have done the same?

—I don't know. What did he say?

—He didn't understand some of the words.

—Is he a foreigner?

—No, he's just plain ignorant.

—Do you remember any of the words?

—Well, they didn't know where Iran was. Anybody who reads the papers would. But because they're old they think they don't have to keep up with the news. I despise them. They're lazy, and selfish. No matter how old I get I'll always keep myself informed. You never know when you'll be needed. When you'll be called on to act.

—I understand . . .

—No, you don't. I haven't stopped reading since I arrived here. Especially after noticing that I could remember all I read. I find it very stimulating.

—But people have a right to retire.

—You just want to antagonize me.

—No, Mr. Ramirez, I think it's wonderful that you keep yourself informed, but you're exceptional. Most elderly people probably don't bother.

—I have very little in common with them. They bore me. Tell me about that woman.

—What woman?

—The one who was so important to you.

—I don't want to discuss it.

—So she was important; you're admitting it.

— . . .

—I read the other day that only what frightens you can make you angry.

—Now you're the one talking like a shrink.

—You *are* frightened.

—Enough, I'm not going to discuss this. You're being a pain in the ass.

—That's not a nice thing to say.

—You deserved it.

—Thanks for your fine manners.

— . . .

—I don't know how, but with all this nonsense we've been talking about, I forgot to tell you something. Something pretty important. You can leave.

—What?

—Well, you see, my nurse is really a nice kid. Today she's going home at three as usual, but then she's coming back. I wasn't going to allow her to do that, you know; she has a family to look after. But, oh no, there was no stopping her, she wanted to come at five, and you know what? She is! She says she enjoys reading to me. We haven't decided yet about a book. Maybe some Jane Austen, or something by the other Brontë girl. Isn't that nice of her?

—Yes, very nice.

—But, Larry, this way, you see, it's not necessary for you to stay two hours; you can leave sooner.

—O.K.

—And you don't have to worry about money; you'll get your full pay. I know you won't charge me for your lunch hours, but you'll be paid for the rest of your time.

—Terrific.

—And now that I think of it, I haven't offered her any money. That's odd of me. I'm sure she could use it. I'll bring up the matter today. She won't be offended, and what a blessing it will be if she accepts! Of course, that leads me to another subject, the impossibility of paying you and her at the same time. But you would understand, wouldn't you?

—Sure.

—We should be realistic about this. Right now, I mean. Because she's going to accept my proposal. So, Larry, you see, I wouldn't have thought of replacing you with any other young man . . . but this girl! You know how sweet she is, and I need her tenderness. So, as strange as it may sound, this is the last time you'll be asked to come. I wish I could say I'm sorry to see you leave, but think who's taking your place! An angel . . .

—Don't you need the committee's approval for this change?

—No.

—They won't like being bypassed.

—It won't be the first time. I didn't ask for their permission to hire you.

—Doesn't the committee know about me?

—The committee believes you're an employee of the home; and the home believes you're an employee of the committee. You were hired directly by me, through the agency, of course. I wanted somebody not connected in any way to the committee. I don't want to be spied on. And I get my allowance weekly.

—What time did you say she was returning?

—At five. So you may leave now, if you want; I'll take a nap in-between. She'll wake me up.

—That's impossible; at five she's taking her kid to a swimming class.

—How do you know?

—We're going to meet afterward, Mr. Ramirez.

—Who's we?

—The Virgo and I. She left me a note in my coat pocket.

—I don't believe it.

—So wait for her, then.

—Where is the swimming class?

—In this neighborhood, two blocks away from her apartment.

—Where is her husband?

—He works late.

—Where is her apartment?

—I'm not sure she would like you to know, Mr. Ramirez.

—Well, maybe I made a mistake because, you see, I have two appointments, and I probably mistook one for the other. A couple of very important officials from the human rights committee in New York are coming to see me. I don't know why. I have nothing to do with their affairs. . . . So maybe I'm seeing them and not the nurse at five.

—Probably.

—Don't tell me I never told you about their visit.

—No, never.

—I feel a little uncomfortable with all this attention. Tell me, Larry: Are you one of those people who adores a lot of attention? Or are you just like me? I don't like much fuss.

—I've never gotten that much attention.

—Anyhow, if that sweet girl also comes, I think they'll like her. Or would it be better to call and tell them not to come today, not to bother themselves just for my sake?

—It would be better if they came.

—No, Larry, look, I'll give you the number and you'll call them, O.K.?

—They're very busy people; better let them keep the appointment.

—You think so? No . . . go call them . . .

—The nurse won't come, Mr. Ramirez.

—Virgos seldom get confused about time and appointments, things of that sort. I'm pretty sure she'll be here by five; you'll see . . . and I'm sure we can get some people at the home to serve us some tea and cake, and what better person could I ask to pour the tea for us? They'll see she's an angel right away. . . . But it's possible that they won't come, that they'll forget about the meeting, busy as they are. Anyhow, I hope they will; it would really be a pity for them to miss the tea and the cake and her. And I'm sure it would be useful for her to meet these people. They may help her career. Influential people . . . by the way, wouldn't it be better for you to go and fetch me a nice cake from a fancy bakery? I wouldn't mind the expense for an occasion such as this.

— . . .

—No, I won't ask you to do that.

— . . .

—It must be humiliating for you, at your age, to run errands.

— . . .

—I'm not worrying, but if I run out of money, I'll just ask her to wait a few days for her salary, until my next allowance arrives. You see, she's not as pressed for money as you; for her this is a luxury, a few extra dollars. She'll spend them on toys for her little girl, who knows.

— . . .

—And something else. I'm going to recommend you to the committee. You must try to get work in your field, history! And stop wasting time with menial jobs.

—Thank you, but I don't want to go back to that profession.

—Why not?

—I don't feel ready.

—What do you mean, "I don't feel ready"?

—I just don't feel ready, period.

—As you wish . . . but to top it all, if the officials leave early this evening, she may still be able to spend a half-hour or so reading to me . . . I know what you're thinking, that I'm insatiable . . . oh, Larry, I think I'm being spoiled. I'm a selfish old man. But, luckily, you won't have to put up with me anymore; you won't have to come back. She will take your place, I'm sure.

—Larry comes through the window at night to scare me.

— . . .

—He's going to show up tonight, just like the other night, totally unexpectedly; and he's going to startle and irritate me as usual.

— . . .

—You're right here, aren't you?

— . . .

—As long as you don't answer you'll keep me on edge; I won't be able to rest.

— . . .

—Larry, you've kept me on my guard for hours, so you won't frighten me with your silly appearances.

— . . .

—Larry, the tension has exhausted me. You've certainly taught me the meaning of the word.

— . . .

—I'm really tired, but I'd like to discuss the meaning of other words, nobler ones.

— . . .

—Larry, are you gone now? Am I alone in this room? If I turned the light on to jot down a note, you might sneak up behind me . . . and even have the nerve to read it.

— . . .

—It's a nice day. Let's go out.

—I have a cold.

—Where? You don't sound as if you do.

—I feel it coming on.

—Fresh air will do you good, Mr. Ramirez.

—Is there a special reason why you want to go out?

—It's easier for me to sit here.

—Is it very cold outside?

—No, it's pleasant. It's cool, but the sun's out. It's better for your health than sitting in here.

—I've heard they're going to fire her.

—Who?

—The nurse, who else?

—Why?

—She's a thief, it seems. And has been prying into people's affairs. Very unpleasant business. She's a snitch, too.

—A snitch?

—Yes, precisely.

—It's her job to keep an eye on the patients.

—Going through their personal papers, is that any way to behave?

—No, it isn't. But maybe she has orders to keep tabs on everyone, Mr. Ramirez.

— . . .

—It's probably the policy of management. Anyhow, it's disgusting.

—It all started with the theft of an insignificant little object, but then they discovered it wasn't her first time. She'd been convicted before. She's turned out to be a shady lady.

—The other day you were in love with her. Just day before yesterday.

—Well, I didn't really know her. But I do now.

—Are they really going to fire her?

—Who knows? What exasperates me most is that people like her sometimes get away with their crimes. Imagine, having to associate with a convicted felon. It's revolting.

—Well, you don't have to have her read to you anymore.

—I certainly won't.

—Tell me more about her crimes.

—You seem to take them lightly. Of course, you know she won't be fired. Somebody must have told you, and you're taking her side. The spy's side.

—Who would care about the politics of people in a nursing home?

—Evidently somebody. And now you're admitting they're investigating politics.

—Besides, you've lied before, Mr. Ramirez.

—How dare you?

—I don't believe the business about the nurse. You invented it all.

—I wish it were a lie; I wish they weren't watching me. I don't know why they do. Maybe it's all very innocent. Just part of the treatment. It makes sense that they would want to know if I'm hiding something from them, would want to know what goes on in my head. But it's all so wrong, the way they approach me. They keep me totally in the dark. You know that, don't you?

—How in the dark?

—They wouldn't tell me what happened before I got out of . . . jail. In Argentina.

—You were in jail?

—It was a mistake on the part of the authorities, that's all I know. They falsely accused me of swindling or something like that. When I was released, my brother sent me here. My doctors are better informed than I, and they probably think I'd be upset were I to know all the details.

—You're afraid you might have done something wrong. You could have; you may have hurt somebody.

—What makes you say that?

—You're always imagining that you're being attacked, that's why.

—Do you know anything, anything certain?

—No.

— . . .

—You're really afraid you did something bad, real bad.

—Larry, if I tell the committee about what's been going on here, I'll have to include you among the suspects. But, of course, I'll need evidence before going to them.

—What's the matter? You don't look well.

—I'm feeling awful.

—Should I get a doctor?

—No. You can go if it's too unpleasant to see me this way.

—O.K., bye . . .

—How can you make fun of me at a moment like this? . . . Oh, please . . .

—Please what?

—Listen . . . before you go . . .

—You're so pale. I think we should call a doctor.

—No, there's nothing he would be able to do.

—Let me see. . . . Your forehead is so cold. Give me your hand. . . . You're freezing!

—Please go now . . . or tell me something to ease the pain.

—Listen, Mr. Ramirez, you're not the only person who's ever harmed someone. I killed a man in Vietnam.

—You said you weren't drafted.

—I was lying.

—Why?

—I didn't want you to think badly of me. I spent two years in the service.

—Was the man you killed someone you knew?

—No, I never learned his name. Our platoon was searching a village. The villagers had left several days before. Only Vietcong should have been there. We had our guns at the ready. Suddenly I felt a presence behind me. I wheeled around and saw a small man in dark clothes . . .

—And I know, he resembled somebody . . .

—No, he was just staring at me. I hate to have people creep up on me like that; so I riddled him with bullets.

—And you immediately recognized him . . .

—No, I'd never seen him before, but when I looked at his corpse, I knew he was not a soldier, just an old villager who probably didn't want to leave his home.

—You were lucky you got to him first; he was probably going to bludgeon you to death.

—Yes, I thought he was going to tear me up.

—That was cruel of you; you should have tried to disarm him.

—There's nothing to discuss; it's survival of the quickest.

—What did you do after that?

—I realized I was wrong, that he meant me no harm.

—Did you cry over his body, over his old carcass?

—No, but I felt shitty.

—What happened that night? Were you able to sleep?

—Yeah, I slept.

—But before you went to bed you went to one of those brothels in Saigon.

—The women were wonderful, Mr. Ramirez. Sleek, bronze, with slits in their dresses, painted faces and teased hair. Made up for the Americans. And sexy. All they thought about was sex and money. It's nice to have a woman who thinks only about sex. And who comes on to you.

—Did you go alone?

—Yes.

—Wasn't one of your superiors also there? Did you get the best girl? Or did the officer?

—I didn't go with anyone.

—What were those shabby rooms like?

—Sometimes there was a mirror on the wall, and I would position the woman and myself in front of the mirror so I could see her back and buttocks while she caressed me. Mr. Ramirez, are you still interested in sex?

—I know it was important, but there are things I cannot understand. I've been reading love scenes, and parts of them make sense to me. I understand that people like to be caressed, but I don't understand other things.

— . . .

—Please tell me more about the girl in the brothel.

—Look, Mr. Ramirez, none of this ever happened. Your chest pain is gone; you can breathe O.K. now, and there is no point in continuing.

—A lie?

—Yeah, a lie. I was never abroad.

— . . .

—A complete fabrication, totally untrue.

—Why?

—Why not? You lied to me about that guy in SoHo.

—But you must know about the officer, your superior, who was there. He must have told you about the girls. And you must tell me.

—No, I invented the whole thing.

—If you slept that night it was thanks to her.

—Mr. Ramirez, I told you, I made the whole thing up.

—She caressed you because she was paid to, but then, and this I don't understand, why did you caress her?

—Looking at her back reflected in the mirror, looking at the back of her head, not feeling her warmth, not seeing her face and her tender expressions . . .

—Why didn't you feel her warmth?

—It's a joy to be face-to-face with someone. And to see your pleasure reflected in the other person's face. But a mirror is more perverse; it allows you to step outside the scene and to see the other person as an object, reduced to a thing, giving up herself all for you, prostrating, emptying herself. That's also exciting.

—Which feeling is stronger?

—You need both.

—But why caress and not just look?

—There's less of a person there when she caresses me.

— . . .

—You don't follow me, do you? It's all about seeing a person reduced to a thing that exists only for you, a slave. I don't know why, but there's pleasure in that; it's exciting.

—And what happens when you touch?

—Maybe we should go to some porn films. They have special facilities for handicapped people these days. We'll just put your chair in the aisle.

—I don't want to see films; I want you to answer my question. I want to know why you need to touch.

—You don't even have to love someone to caress her, just like her a little. A caress has a momentum of its own.

—Is the caress you give like the one you receive, or are they different?

—The same.

—I still don't know why one goes around touching others.

— . . .

—It was very nice of you to let the other guy, the officer, go with that girl first.

—There we go again.

—You just said that you didn't know where the brothel was, and that a superior of yours took you there, or was it the other way around? You know, you must be patient with me, I forget things easily.

—You also invent things easily.

—Now you're trying to get me confused. The girl was unmistakably the best one in the brothel. And you let him go first. It shows you have a sense of camaraderie.

—Look, I didn't have a superior, and I didn't go to brothels.

—I once asked my doctor about those feelings.

—What did he say?

—He asked me to think of times when I'm very hungry. But that's almost never. He told me to think of very appetizing food and that I could finally eat as much as I wanted because that would put me to sleep. I'd plunge into deep, refreshing sleep. Or to think of times when I'm thirsty and that I could finally drink my favorite wine, which, too, would put me to sleep. But I'm also never terribly thirsty. I feel only pain that subsides or intensifies.

—Mr. Ramirez, would you like me to take you to a prostitute? You could account for it as a pharmaceutical expense.

—I guess before one visits a prostitute, one must remember what desire is like.

— . . .

—What should one think about on such occasions? What does one do to stop thinking, as the doctor said?

—Actually, that's not a problem. It's not that you stop thinking or that your mind goes blank, but that your usual concerns and worries vanish. You stop planning, and images float through your mind trailed by others.

—Which images come first?

—Sometimes I see in my mind various places I've visited over the years. Memories flood me, things I thought I'd forgotten. My defenses crumble. It's a very pleasing sensation, to give yourself over to that rush.

—Please describe one of your landscapes.

—Hills, rolling hills, and greenery and lakes.

—Is it cold there? Is there wind?

—The climate is always perfect. Comfortable, soothing.

—Have you seen this landscape in paintings or photographs?

—No, in actuality. It's one of the places I've visited outside the city.

—Name one.

—The dunes of Cape Cod. I've traveled very little.

—And who is usually present in the landscape? Are you in it?

—Sometimes I see only the landscape; sometimes I'm in it.

—What are you doing in it?

—Ummm . . . I'm not doing anything; it's just a picture, an image, shapes and colors. And I keep imagining variations, that's the pleasure.

—When I asked you what you did in your vision, you couldn't answer right away; and then you sounded slightly irritated.

—I'm not irritated; it's just difficult to relate what's on my mind.

—What is the final landscape you see before falling asleep?

—Sometimes I also dream landscapes. Those are always very pleasant dreams. The landscape is then like the body of a woman you're exploring.

—Try to concentrate and tell me about the last landscape you see before you fall asleep.

—Enough of this; I can't think about this anymore.

—Would it be possible for you to explain to me what you feel in your member at such moments?

—It's not only there; the feeling floods your whole body. It's . . . I don't know how to explain . . .

—Try to make an effort.

—What's the point?

—Since you can't explain what you feel, could you at least tell me what it resembles? Something I might experience or remember in my present condition?

—Have you ever gone swimming?

—Not recently; but I remember what it was like, I don't know why.

—When the water is not too warm, not too cold, but just right, and you've been swimming, and you emerge into the open air, and beads of water glisten on your body, and your skin begins to tingle; that's how I feel during sex.

—I remember those sensations, but they weren't so terribly important to me as, I see, they are to most people. It's their importance that I can't understand.

—After you're through, even if you don't love the person, you find that you care in some way, even if you started out indifferent or resentful or annoyed.

—That's your version of sex and I don't understand most of it. But if you'd be so kind, I would like to know what that other guy felt in the brothel.

— . . .

—You both wanted the best girl. Was it terribly painful for you to lose her to him? What was the difference between her and the other girls?

— . . .

—Why was she better?

— . . .

—Could she stand improvement? Did you like her exactly as she was?

—You mean the person you really desire? The one who knocks you out? When she appears, your sexual impulse is checked a little. And you're in a daze, sort of transfixed by this magical object.

—But then you attain her.

—No, never. You can have all the others easily, but you're always longing for her. The person you really want, who, if you had her, would solve so many problems, fill so many gaps, heal so many wounds. She is virtually unattainable; you weaken as you approach her.

—But the moment comes when you have her. I want to

remember, because I know I attained her. If I only could remember, I wouldn't mind not having her here now.

— . . .

—Do you believe me when I say I attained her?

—No.

—Why?

—I think it's an illusion. That someone or something that could make us whole.

—What made the girl in the brothel perfect?

— . . .

—If you don't remember her too well, think of another woman you found extraordinary and who couldn't be any better.

— . . .

—Do you remember imagining at that moment an unsurpassable landscape?

— . . .

—Have you forgotten it?

—What impresses you is what that landscape symbolizes.

—Larry, is the landscape itself not enough?

—It stands for something. I think it stands for something.

—What were the dunes in Cape Cod substitutes for?

—If a woman is perfect you can hardly approach her. She's so perfect, such a goddess, that it's almost hubristic for one to imagine her directly; therefore, all these images, substitutions, etc.

—You cannot be intent on something so desperately unless you have known it before. It's not true that you were never with her. You were, and you lost her. I know, because I don't care to get what I didn't have before. What's happened to you is that you don't remember her, just as I can't remember so many other things. You had her and you lost her, you just don't remember.

— . . .

—Those dunes, can you recall them perfectly?

—I used to love to explore them, to climb the mountains and walk through the valleys, to wade through the swampy parts. There's nothing like exploring new terrain. I always have the urge to survey it, to draw a map, to chart it, as if I had discovered it and were its first explorer.

—You haven't answered my question. Do you remember those dunes, perfectly or not?

—No.

—Why not?

— . . .

—It seems as if you don't want to continue the discussion. But if you won't help me, who will?

— . . .

—Silence makes me ill.

— . . .

—And you still don't want to tell me about the officer in Saigon.

—I hope I never become a crotchety old man.

—You know something, your memory is worse than mine. You have already told me all about your pal, that night you were ashamed that he saw you at that place. And you had had deep respect for him before because he was older and of higher rank. And he sort of respected you, too.

— . . .

—It's useless to evade it. It happened and we are all responsible for our acts. But if you didn't tell me the truth when you first told the story, now is the time to set the record straight. You arrived at the brothel by yourself; it was your first time; the directions you'd gotten were vague and the road tortuous, but you finally got there. The officer himself had given you directions; so why were you so surprised to find him there?

—This man has whorehouses on the brain. Mr. Ramirez, did you used to frequent them?

—That's exactly what you said to the officer when he

suggested taking you there. That's why you didn't like bumping into him at the place.

—All right, so we are in this brothel, now what happens?

—You saw him drinking a glass of wine.

—Rice wine.

—He was there waiting; you found that out afterward. You heard that chant you told me about; you heard it in the distance. And you wanted to find out where it was coming from. You were bold and opened a door; it led into a dark corridor. Then you heard the music better. There were rooms, very small rooms with their doors ajar, and dark, no, in some there were tiny candles burning. The occupants were mostly old people, lying on cots, each alone, looking very unhappy, though all were having opium dreams.

—What kind of music was playing? Was it an Argentine tango?

—No, you told me it was Chinese, very refined and delicate, almost religious. And you continued walking; at the end of the corridor was a beaded curtain.

—What was behind the curtain, Mr. Ramirez?

—It was a much better room, but you could barely see the pillows outlined against a paper wall. Now the music got louder, you had to walk carefully; there seemed to be something strange stretched out on the pillows. The only light was coming from behind the wall, or was it a paper screen?

—Was there smoke from the opium pipes?

—Yes, you told me the smell was . . . what was it you told me?

—Second-rate Colombian marijuana.

—You thought it was marijuana. But it was really much more dangerous.

—Cigarettes.

—No, they were the little rubber balls that you burn; I read about them in the encyclopedia. And there was a drawing of an opium den very similar to the one you told me about. Then I don't know, maybe it was fear of those snakes that seemed to crawl among the pillows, or maybe you didn't want to flatter yourself, and what you really did was tear up the paper screen, burst through, because you couldn't wait any longer to see her. You had a hunch that she was there, the most beautiful girl in the brothel. The officer had told you about her. Were you disappointed when you saw her, or was she as spectacular as he had said? Did you find her flawed in any way?

—A few beauty marks.

—But by then it was too late. You heard steps behind you and it was the officer. He had been waiting for her all night, but she hadn't come out, and you remembered it was thanks to him that you had found the place, so you were grateful and let him have her first.

—Yeah, I let him have her first. Warts and all. One of her breasts was withered and discolored.

—After he had her?

—No.

—It wasn't worth killing him just to have her to yourself, was it?

—Did I kill him?

—No, of course not. But what was so special about her, or better, what was so inferior about the other girls?

—They stunk afterward, like rubber or fish. Did you ever smell cunt that's been fucked? There's nothing like it. I always have to take a shower after fucking to get the stench off me. You have to soap up two or three times. It smells like something rotting, putrefying, decaying, like mildew. They should bottle the scent and use it to revive people who have fainted. Mr. Ramirez, do you remember the smell of cunt?

—It was as if the officer had had a revelation. There was no evidence of danger at all, but somehow he thought it was better to wait for you, and get back to camp together. The air inside that hovel was unbearable; he walked into the jungle night. Everything was still; there was no breeze, but at least he didn't have to watch those faces. He was waiting for you, hiding behind a tree.

—What was he going to do?

—He may have been jealous, and that was a perfect occasion to get rid of you. Some guerrilla could have been posted there, the enemy would have been blamed.

—You mean gotten the credit.

— . . .

—Did they shoot me or not?

—If the officer hadn't been there, they surely would have. He was hiding just to surprise you, to give you a fright, but when you finally came out he saw strange shadows moving in the tropical foliage, and it couldn't have been the swaying of palm trees because there was no wind. He shouted so you would duck. And you did. The bullets of the enemy couldn't reach you. You heard them flee. And you were safe. Thanks to him.

— . . .

—It's time for you to leave, isn't it, Larry?

—Maybe; it doesn't matter, though.

—Please, I'm going to ask you to do me a favor.

—What?

—Please go and eat at the restaurant tomorrow, our restaurant. Here's the money.

—Why?

—I can't go, I don't feel well enough. But if you go you'll be able to tell me all about it, and that would help, believe me. You know I'm peculiar sometimes.

—Come in.

—How are you feeling, Mr. Ramirez?

—Isn't it Tuesday? What are you doing here?

—Well, I heard you were sick, and I thought I'd drop by to see how you were.

—Did she tell you I was in bed?

—I called you earlier, but the receptionist said you couldn't be brought to the phone because you were ill.

— . . .

—I called to change the hours for tomorrow. I have a job interview.

—I see . . .

—I'm applying for a job as a research assistant at Columbia University . . .

—Would you start working right away? How many hours a week?

—I would start in a few months.

—I'm feeling awfully cold, you know. My blood pressure has dropped, and I keep breaking out in a cold sweat. My armpits are all wet at this moment, and my feet, though they're frozen, are wet, too. I'm so disgusted with myself . . . I can't stand it any longer. I smell. And I can't take more than one shower a day; it weakens me too much.

—I'm sorry.

—Don't get any closer. Leave your coat there. I don't want you to smell me.

—It's all right, I don't mind perspiration.

—If I don't get better I'll be taken to the hospital tomorrow.

—What's wrong with you? You were fine yesterday.

—If I'm taken to a hospital the shrinks will think they were right in not telling me all I want to know.

—I don't follow you.

—For them the important thing is to keep me unaware.

— . . .

—And I need to know. Not to be treated as a wreck who couldn't take one more blow.

—How much have the doctors told you about what happened before you came to this country?

—Very little. That I was jailed by mistake; I hadn't swindled anybody. Then the plane trip and a hospital in this country two days later. That's all.

—Do you know what happened while you were in jail?

—No.

—Would you like to know?

—I won't improve otherwise.

—But don't denounce me afterward.

—Whatever you do is my responsibility, Larry. Don't forget I hired you without anybody's permission.

—O.K., I'll tell you what I know.

— . . .

— . . .

—I'm listening . . . why aren't you talking?

—I agree with you, they're wrong to treat you as a mental . . . case.

—I'm listening.

—Your family was killed.

—How do you know?

—Well, where are they now?

—Who told you that?

—The nurse. I asked her. And she's not very professional.

—Larry . . . she told me she knew nothing.

—She didn't want to upset you. I don't want to upset you either. Perhaps you don't want to know.

—Tell me everything she said! Please!

—Lie back and try to relax. You said it would help you if you knew; I think so, too. But you must calm down.

—I can't!

— . . .

—But, please . . . repeat all she said.

—All right. Your family was killed.

—How?

—A bomb was planted in your house. It happened when you were already in jail. But for political reasons, not for swindling.

—The doctors want to cheer me up. Trying to make me believe that. But I won't let them fool me so easily. I hope it was all true.

—What? What I'm telling you is cheering you up?

—I don't know what that feels like. But it's certainly not the worst possible news that a bomb killed them. That is, if I had a family.

—Aren't you ashamed to say so? Wouldn't you prefer it if they were alive?

—No.

—Why not?

—I don't know . . . because then . . . they might be suffering. They could be paying for my faults.

—Which ones?

—I don't remember. But you, why do you want to know? Somebody's sent you to pry!

—The swindle was an invention of yours. Your brother was an invention.

—Two years ago I was a strong man, the doctors themselves told me.

—Then you don't believe what I just said.

—I have my reasons . . . not to.

—Tell me, Mr. Ramirez.

— . . .

—Somewhere within you, you know what really happened. I don't have to tell you.

—Oh yes, you do. Please. You must repeat to me all the

lies she told you. Who did she say was killed? What sort of family did they invent for me?

—Your wife, your son and your daughter-in-law.

—I know I once lived with a woman. We went to the seashore, a place with dunes. But I never had children.

—I told you because that's what she told me. I figured the truth might help.

—Larry, believe me, I'm sorry. I don't like to be depressing . . . with the spectacle of my misery.

—You shouldn't be perspiring like that. Why don't we call a doctor?

—No . . . but before you go, I want you to listen to this . . . I think it was unkind of you, that date with the nurse. But I bear no resentments. You're young; I've been reading about the urges you people feel, and how you're slaves to them.

—Nothing happened with the nurse. It's not very easy for young people either. It's not always easy to get together.

—But you had a date with her.

—Well, nothing happened. And even if something had, so what? Why are you complaining about the sex drive of young people? You're always talking about it. You speak as if it were evil, selfish.

—If you're telling me that nothing happened in order to make me feel better, it won't work.

—Mr. Ramirez, I think you're a voyeur. Would you like me to set a little something up for you, so that you can hear some grunts and groans in the room next to yours? I'm sure your spirits would be revived.

—I'm not interested in the mechanics. I want to know what goes on inside a person. What did you feel when you saw her waiting for you that evening? Or didn't she keep the appointment?

—What about the news I just gave you about your family? Isn't that more important?

—I had no such family. Continue.

—Don't you prefer to discuss something . . . so essential to you?

—Those are only fabrications of yours, so as not to tell me about the nurse.

— . . .

— . . .

—Your wish is my command. Where were we? Yes . . . there're so many variables during these rendezvous. A thousand things have to happen for one to go right. What if one person is in one mood, the other in a different mood? Or one is buoyant and expansive, the other a little down and needy?

—I don't want to hear about rendezvous; I want to hear about your date with the nurse.

— . . .

—Please . . .

—Will you get better if I tell you?

—I promise . . .

—You promise what?

—To do everything possible to get better, all that's in my power.

—You're like a vampire. You feed on other people's lives. Try to imagine how the victim feels, who is steadily drained.

—There's only one victim here, and that's me. A victim of poor health and poor medical care.

— . . .

—Larry, what is so shameful about what happened that night?

—Nothing happened, only strained conversation.

—How long was her daughter's swimming lesson?

—An hour.

—She was going to take you to her apartment two blocks away. Her husband was working nights. You told me all that. Where did you spend that hour?

—We sat in a coffee shop.

—Why didn't you go to her apartment?

—I wasn't sure I wanted to.

—She's very attractive.

—Yeah.

—What did you talk about?

—All kinds of things. Such conversations generally skirt the issue. You can talk about a thousand-and-one topics, world events, other people, but the hardest thing to talk about is one's own feelings and needs in relation to the other person. It's never directly said, only obliquely hinted at. Suggestions, innuendos, flirtation. Flirtation and repression go hand-in-hand, and there has to be repression in order to derive pleasure from flirtation.

—I don't understand. When you left that night you were expecting something else to happen. I could see that you desired her strongly, and you didn't mind pushing me out of your way. You were blinded by that urge. And she was taking you to her apartment. That's why I'm not going to believe your version. You don't want me to know that people get what they want out of life.

— . . .

—You got what you wanted, confess.

—Sometimes people are satisfied; not always.

—Did she? I mean, did she only want to flirt and feel desired?

—She wanted that, and something more.

—What?

—Sex and affection.

—What did you want?

—The same thing.

—What you're not telling me is that the two of you met again the following day.

—I love your imagination. There was no second time, once was enough. I find it very awkward to be with somebody I desire unless I'm in the process of having her.

—You were only two blocks away from having her, why did you let her stop you?

—She didn't. I stopped myself. I tend to sabotage these affairs. There's a way of doing it, a way of shattering the mood, these moods where two people feel warm and responsive toward each other. They're fragile, and can be broken by simply discussing . . . some factual matter.

—What did you feel when you finally embraced her, once you were in her apartment?

—I told you, I never embraced her. And I wish my life were as vivid as your imagination. If I get to the point where I'm in bed with a woman or holding her, then there's no problem. The problem is before. Somehow when you're open and express your needs you're vulnerable, if they're either not met or rejected.

—You're not as attractive as you think, but you're not a monster. Who rejected you and why?

—I don't know; I always felt this way.

—I must know when it hurt most, and where you felt the pain.

—You're a pain in the ass.

—That's gross. . . . Was the pain in your eyes? My eyes once felt as if they were filled with burning ice.

—When was that?

—The night the nurse waited for you outside the gym.

— . . .

—When did you hurt most?

—Why did you feel rejected, Mr. Ramirez? I was going to see you the next day.

—But she wasn't coming to see me that night. She had chosen you.

— . . .

—The same ice slowly penetrates and deadens my brain. My lungs continue to function for one more hour, and my

73

heart. I'll be tortured, but I won't be able to think, won't be able to know what's killing me.

— . . .

—I hope this sounds strange to you, something alien happening to an old man. Tell me you never felt this bad in your life, as if you were going to die.

—But I have. And it was worse, because I knew I was not going to die.

—But, Larry, if you feel you're going to die, you feel you're losing everything. There's nothing worse than that.

—Enough! You absurd old man! A minute ago you told me your relatives would be better off dead; but you yourself don't want to die.

—I can defend myself. Maybe they couldn't. If they were killed, it's because they didn't know how to defend themselves. In this world I can defend myself.

—And you can pester people, too. Sometimes you're more like a whining child than a man who has lived for seventy-four years.

—Then . . . you never think of diseases like gangrene and the other infections, the ones caused by cold weather?

—Never.

—That means you're healthy. Maybe the biggest fear you've known in your life has been not knowing whether you'd make it to the end of the month.

—That's very unpleasant.

—Larry, can I ask you a favor?

—It depends.

—Tell me what you see when you close your eyes and pretend that you're terribly afraid. Maybe I could try to see the same thing when fear overcomes me.

—You want to know my defenses?

—I want to know your enemies; I'll try to think of them as mine. Close your eyes and tell me what they're like. They seem almost tame.

—. . .

—Do you see houses? Houses you've been in? People? People you know?

—. . .

—What do they do to you? Who's there to defend you? Who betrays you after pretending to be your friend?

—O.K. One of my worst fears is of no longer being attractive, of no longer being able to use my looks. Perhaps you have known this fear. How did you get past the point when you were no longer attractive? How were you able to feel good about yourself? That you still had a life to lead, that your life had some meaning, that there were still pleasures to enjoy? What was it like, and how did you get over the hump?

—I'm poor; I can't give you much; I can't give you anything; I know nothing.

—. . .

—All I have . . . all I cherish is the hope of finding my notes.

—Don't try that pathetic bit with me again. You're putting too much emphasis on those notes. It's not going to come from the outside, it's all in your head. Your brain isn't damaged.

—Describe the face, there's somebody declaring that he's your friend; you're walking side by side; but then . . . then . . . he steps back and you turn around and you see a knife in his hand.

—It happens all the time. People retreat from intimacy, from exposing themselves even a little, from feeling attached. They need to, but they're afraid. I do it all the time. I always step back.

—Oh no, not you, Larry.

—Always.

—Does the other man, the one behind you, have your face then?

—I don't know what you're talking about.

—What's the face like, the face of the man behind you, the man holding the knife?

— . . .

—Never mind. I've asked you sufficient questions, haven't I? And I had forgotten that you're here as a visitor today, not an attendant. Thank you, don't think for a moment that I don't appreciate what you've done.

—It's nothing, I was close by and I thought I'd drop in.

—That's not the important point. You came here to tell me that nothing had happened between you and the nurse, so I wouldn't feel left out. . . . You took the trouble to invent a whole story just for my sake.

—I didn't lie.

—Well, it's useless trying to fool me. She was here before you, and she gave me the true version of what happened. The nurse said she saw you coming toward her. Then you stopped at the corner. She was happy to see you and didn't hide it.

— . . .

—She saw you. And then you couldn't make up your mind whether to cross the street or not.

—It's bad enough when you lose a person in your life, but then everything else loses its meaning.

—You didn't know whether to cross the street or not. Maybe then you closed your eyes. Was it dark? Was the street well lit?

—At such times you don't notice the street. The pain spreads like cancer, devouring everything. It goes away during sleep, but a few seconds after you wake up, it comes back. And yet I've never considered killing myself. I wonder why. A pain so deep it destroys the meaning of life. There must be meaning in suffering. As painful and horrible as it is, there must be a need it satisfies. In its presence thoughts of suicide don't arise; and it keeps you locked in one position.

—She told me she felt reassured and comfortable with you right away, in the coffee shop, and that . . .

—Shut up! Will you? When my girl friend left me, it was like having my skin peeled off. I felt so anxious; yet I put up a front, pretended it didn't matter to me at all. I was in the house calmly reading, while she was packing her things. She was very anxious, too, she was falling apart. Both of us were. She needed to leave me, but she wanted me to say "Stay, don't go." So she picked fights with me, over who was to get what. As I let her have more, conceded more and more things, she got extravagant and wanted everything. I became so unresponsive that the only way she could get to me was by attacking me. But I kept my cool, not giving in, refusing to say "Stay, I need you." I think that was the difficult thing. To say "I need you. I'm weak without you." That much I couldn't admit. So I treated it as a minor incident, my separation from the woman I had lived with for so many years. Like losing a cat.

—Did you open your eyes then? Or were you still waiting to cross the street?

— . . .

—You mustn't be afraid anymore; you have forgotten all about that evening, but it doesn't matter because I remember and I can tell you.

—Tell me, what happened?

—Maybe it was just a word, a phrase. But when she heard it, the nurse knew she had to throw her husband out. Just one word and you had a home waiting for you. A warm, cozy place with a woman you wanted.

—It sounds stifling. I don't want to live there.

—Larry, you said the man who was behind you had your face. How do I know that it's you and not he who is here with me now?

—I don't understand a word of what you've said.

—You told me a short while ago, only this afternoon. And, oh! I remember something else: one day in the park you told me the other one's voice was vicious. And I couldn't describe the sound of yours now with a better word.

—I'm not angry with you yet.

—If you are, tell me who once hit you with the piece of a two-by-four.

—My father.

—The vicious voice. . . . Well, if you don't know I'll tell you. Larry never suffered any rejection, while you . . . you can't think of anything but that.

—You're mistaken. He knew rejection, too. When he was seventeen, his mother threw him out; he had no job, no money; he wasn't going to school, he had no place to go.

—No, you're mistaken. It wasn't his mother, it was his father who threatened Larry.

—No, his father was full of threats and rage, but couldn't act decisively, and wouldn't have thrown the kid out. Only his mother was strong enough to do something like that. The fights with her started as soon as he reached puberty.

—Impossible. The nurse told me everything; Larry would never pick a fight, least of all with a woman.

—One day, early in the morning, I called on my friend Charlie to play stickball. I was wearing sneakers, a T-shirt and the baggy dungarees that my mother always bought me. I carried my stick on my shoulder. I was a very skinny kid with a mop of hair. So I'm walking down the block and I see this young woman going to work, probably to an office because of how she was dressed. She was wearing high-heeled shoes and the hem of her skirt was just a little below her knees. High heels tense the muscles in women's calves; they tend to make them strut like horses. My eyes alighted on her calves, the muscles, the curves; but it was her shape that aroused me. All of a sudden I felt something stirring in my pants; I didn't know what was happening; I thought maybe something was wrong. I was surprised and a little frightened, but I followed the woman to the bus stop and watched her mount the bus.

—I remember Larry telling me the same story. And how he showed his erection to his mother. She kissed him on his forehead, and told him not to worry; he was becoming a healthy young man.

—The ideal mother, huh? That's all we need.

—Yes, ideal. Unlike yours.

—Yes, unlike mine. I didn't tell anybody about it. Not even the boys. I was too embarrassed, ashamed, afraid they might laugh. It wasn't something I felt I could tell anyone; it was something I had to live with myself. And it's always been that way.

—Your mother saw you were hiding your erection, and that made her mad.

—I didn't play stickball that day. I went back home, and waited for it to go down. I became very aware of my clothes, of how baggy and ugly they were. And I wanted to get rid of my stick, to wear a suit and follow the woman on the bus. I didn't know her, she was taller and much older than I, and the difference between us made me feel a little ridiculous.

—That's when you started trying to look like Larry, and, for a moment, you can fool whomever you want. But only for a moment. . . . Larry's gone. I left him an envelope at the director's office. With a note and a few dollars so he can eat what he pleases.

—I saw him at a shabby pizza parlor.

—When?

—Years ago.

—Where?

—In Manhattan.

—Where in Manhattan?

—Thirty-fourth Street.

—What was he doing there?

—Eating pizza.

—Don't be stingy with words.

—I think it was a piece of Sicilian pizza, maybe with mushrooms, on a greasy piece of wax paper. Oil was dripping off the ends; he had tomato sauce around his mouth.

—Why was he on Thirty-fourth Street?

—He left home and was looking for a place to stay.

—He was only seventeen.

—Right, he was seventeen.

—He had left home because a girl might have been waiting for him. The kind of adventure you expect at his age. While you, it was your mother who threw you away. Like garbage.

—Yes, it was. We'd been having trouble for four or five years. Ever since puberty. She had a lot of problems with that. It wasn't just the lustful thoughts and perversions she attributed to me, but the whole idea of freedom tied up with sexuality.

—I know that mothers bathe their babies. When does that stop? At what age?

—Well, when the mother first becomes attracted to the little boy's body and genitals. Father's away at work; all the men in her life are at work. And there's only one little man around, who has been bathed and cared for and nurtured for years. It's impossible for this attachment not to have a sexual component. And what effect does it have on the boy who feels it, who has his mother to himself for most of the day? His father comes home at night and eats and sleeps with her; and that's a little mysterious, but for most of the day she belongs to the boy. And he wonders why she even agrees to spend time with his father, who's such a lug. The little man feels superior to his father. The father is only on the scene by virtue of his size and age. He's the usurper, and has to be annihilated. Every night he comes home and sleeps with Mother in the bedroom, the little boy must go to his own room. All the furniture in my mother's bedroom fascinated me, the mirror, the mahogany wood, the brass candles, the perfume bottles in the glass tray, the pictures around the edge of the mirror, the tassels on the bedspread, her underwear in her chest, her powder box, bobby pins and sachets and towels and slips and slippers and the rug and the parquet floor. I wanted her body, but didn't know it. She didn't let me into her bedroom too often. Sometimes when we went to the beach I had to zip up her bathing suit. It zipped up in the back, a long zipper starting at just above her buttocks. She would hug the front of the bathing suit to her breasts, and the straps would be loose. I would zip up the back, and I would do it as slowly as I could. If I was feeling bold I would pull the suit out a little ways to get a grip on it, and then zip her up. I could then see the beginning of her crack, her buttocks, and the beautiful curve in the small of her back. Sometimes in the summer, when it was very hot, she would wear a loose blouse and no bra. She would often sit at the kitchen table and read the newspaper. I would stand on a chair behind her, pretending I was reading along, but looking down her blouse, at her nipples, dark brown and big. Can you imagine! And not being able to touch her.

—Larry's such a good friend of yours he must have told you what happened afterward.

—We were very close, but it all turned sour. I became unruly, cocky; stayed out till four in the morning; got drunk, smoked, read philosophy, novels, and all that upset her. And it was unbearable for me there, but people who fight are deeply attached, and it was a real rupture for me to leave. But I didn't show any emotion, I was cool. She was more upset about it than I was. We fought and fought and fought, and when she said go, I said O.K., and started to pack my duffel bag. I was cracking inside, but defiant.

—Where did you stay that night?

—The first night I slept in the subway. Riding the E train

back and forth. It's possible to sleep sitting up without falling over. As you begin to slump, you jerk your head and shoulders up while sleeping. Your brain is still in touch with reality. Sometimes the conductor would wake me up at the last stop and I would have to take another train.

— . . .

—It had been going on for six months with my wife. I mentioned her to you before, the woman I lived with. It happened after ten years of marriage. It took about six to nine months to come to a head. And after we had spent a month vacationing together. It was impossible. She started to have affairs. Her idea, she told me later, was not to leave, but to have affairs so she could endure our relationship. She wanted me to leave: She'd provoke me, wake me up at night, get drunk, turn off the TV when I was watching. To force me to break up with her. Painful as it was, I didn't leave her.

— . . .

—And now I remember something else my mother said: "If you come back after eight o'clock, you'll find the door locked." That was as unreasonable as saying don't go out. I was dressed to kill; I had a date; I felt like a man; and I wasn't going to be shackled by a stupid rule. I acted defiantly, without regard to the consequences. When I came home at about eleven, the door was locked and chained, I couldn't open it with my key, so fuck-you-I'll-sleep-out, I took the bus to the subway and slept on a train all night.

—You lie; first you mentioned a duffel bag and now it's nowhere to be found.

—As I talk about it, I remember more and more. It was the next day that I was thrown out for good. Now she had justification. It was almost as if she was easing herself into it, step by step. First one night, and then forever. She had to get rid of me, because of some conflict my freedom, my so-called wildness, was causing her. I wasn't really wild; that was her term. I can hardly speak and think without using her language. I was just a normal adolescent, feeling his vitality.

—Larry, please, repeat more of your mother's words.

— . . .

—Is your memory failing?

—It wasn't only words, but attitudes. Or reactions that were automatic, unthinking.

—I'm feeling tired, I can't deal with ideas anymore. Just give me a few of her words.

—They weren't hers, either. She didn't have thoughts of her own. Her own needs, which were different from mine, didn't find language to express themselves, were just a nagging pressure.

—I'm too tired, I can't follow you. But if you repeat her words . . . maybe . . . I'll . . . be able . . . to understand.

— . . .

—You can't repeat them . . . because you don't remember.

— . . .

—You can't remember what Larry's mother said . . . because . . .

— . . .

—You can fool people some of the time but not all of the time.

— . . .

—I never asked you to come here. Please go . . .

— . . .

—I told you to leave.

—See you tomorrow.

—Thanks for leaving the envelope with the money.

—Larry . . . you really scared me . . .

—You didn't hear me come in?

—No.

—The night is silent. How could you not hear my footsteps?

—You came once again through the window, like a phantom.

—I'm sorry, Mr. Ramirez.

—Through carefully locked doors and windows.

—I have more urgent things to discuss with you. Mr. Ramirez, I didn't tell you this before because I was afraid that you'd make fun of me. But now I'm sure you'll be able to understand.

—My limitations are notorious, but I'll give you my utmost attention. Have a seat.

—Thank you. It happened the night of my date with the nurse, shortly after I left that oppressive café. I was alone. I had chosen to walk down a dark street, to immerse everything in darkness. There wasn't a soul in sight; a freezing wind made the bare branches creak. I had to walk carefully; some of the snow in the streets had turned to slippery, treacherous ice.

—A shadow appeared at the corner. It turned and walked in your direction.

—Yes, it was several feet ahead of me.

—It was a woman.

—She was wearing a full-length fur coat with a hood. And boots. She was walking very slowly.

—Somewhat stooped.

—In spite of her coat I could see her waist. A narrow waist. Girted by a leather strap. I knew she was young even before I saw her face, maybe because of the way she swung her arms.

—No one could hear your footsteps. You were as quiet as an assailant.

—She was walking slowly; sooner or later I was going to pass her if she kept going in the same direction. It disturbs me to have somebody walk behind me, and she too would have been startled had she suddenly seen me by her side.

—You stretched your arm out for something.

— . . .

—Yes, Larry, the world is full of things and young people must reach out for them.

—She heard me; she turned around. She kept walking, but soon stopped. She raised her arms as if to protect herself. I cried out that she had nothing to fear. She started to tremble. Then she fainted. What should I have done, Mr. Ramirez?

—You went to her rescue; you raised her by her arms. But in spite of your reassuring words, your shaking her gently, she didn't respond. Finally, you carried her in your arms. You knocked at a door.

—A door with a shiny brass knocker. A light went on in the nearest window and an unfriendly face observed us. He shook his head signifying no. He was an old man like you, with little patience. The light went out. The door wasn't opened.

—I would have opened it.

—Possibly. But you have no house of your own.

—Where did you eventually take her?

—Mr. Ramirez, I blush at the mere mention of what happened afterward. I could have carried her in my arms to the avenue, and waited for a taxi there. But at that moment I blacked out. Yes, I was immersed in darkness; I'd attained my purpose. I had forgotten my name and many other things. The taxi driver would never have been able to guess my address. No light flashed in my mind. But something made me keep walking in the same direction. A block farther I came to an abandoned pier on the Hudson. Sometimes homeless beggars camp there. They build fires, to keep warm. A fire at the abandoned pier. The woman wasn't heavy, but I had to move carefully on the ice. I was out of breath when I reached the crumbling warehouse. I've pointed it out to you during one of our walks.

—Yes, the huge warehouse by the pier, half-destroyed by arson.

—And subsequently abandoned. And that night it was submerged in total darkness. In the woman's handbag there was a cigarette lighter. I used it to light some newspapers that were lying on the ground; I rolled them into a torch. In a corner I found two broken old chairs and pieces of wood, which the bums used to keep fires going. Soon I'd made a fire. The woman was lying on the dirty cement floor, but her skin wasn't touching the filth; gloves, boots, a hooded coat protected her. She was still unconscious. I brought her closer to the fire, I sat on the floor and put her head in my lap. The warm air that almost enveloped her brought an expression of comfort to her face, even pleasure. Then she opened her eyes.

—She asked where she was, showing no anxiety.

—Yes. But then she immediately asked who I was. The only thing, absolutely the only thing that I could remember at that moment was the strained scene between the nurse and me at the café. "Who are you?" she asked me, and I answered the only way I could: "I saw you in the street, walking feebly; I saw you faint. I was coming from a quite unfortunate meeting; I understood very well the way you were feeling. All your strength had also been sapped." She asked again who I was.

—Describe the woman, please. Her face.

—When she spoke her sincerity and decency were evident.

—That's very important.

—Do you think so? . . . Well, when my turn came to ask her who she was, she became vague, as before. She remembered everything, I'm sure, but could say nothing. "I've promised, under oath, not to reveal the secret." What secret? I asked myself. Then I spoke nonsense, said she didn't want to talk to get even with me for my silence. I asked her if my silence offended her. She said she didn't have time for such games because she had to act without further delay. But she needed my help. And yes, it really mattered to her, whether I was willing to help her or not. I answered yes, without thinking that I was in no condition to help her. But the anticipation of vertigo put an end to all useless reflection. She needed to go back to that dark street where I had found her, not far from where I live. I put the fire out to avoid being seen from a distance. She had arrived at the door of a certain house before, but hadn't found the courage to enter. She was retreating when I found her.

—Didn't it startle you when you arrived with her at the appointed door only to discover that it was the entrance to your apartment building?

—It looked like it, but it wasn't.

—That's what you told yourself, to calm your growing terror.

—Along the way she had explained what we had to do. Inside the apartment were her documents and jewelry, and some money. She had to get them back. Before the return of the man she feared so much. Then she would go far away from the city, without leaving any trace behind her.

—Who was the man?

—She refused to say. Once in front of the door she swooned again. The cold and the fear had robbed her of her equilibrium once more. I held her. She said it was better not to try to do anything; the man could be inside the house, waiting for her. I answered that if that were the case I would defend her. The man couldn't attack her if I intervened.

—The man could have had a gun.

—I asked her whose house it was. She didn't answer. I guessed then that it was the man's house, and that we were entering it like thieves. She asked me to trust her as she had trusted me from the moment she found herself in my arms by the fire.

—When you opened the door, you saw the usual roaches, Larry, the old grease dripping from the stove, stalactites of disgusting grease and filth.

—Nothing was in sight. She preferred not to put the light on, she was going to find all she needed just by touch.

—The mattress was lying on the floor; she could have tripped and fallen.

—She proceeded with determination. She led me by the hand, like a blind man. I heard her opening drawers, searching everything, to no avail. Then she took me to another corner, she opened a sliding door. There were clothes hanging there; she seemed to search through them one by one. She told me, in the softest whisper, that all her efforts had been useless. She was standing beside me, and, easily, I reached out and embraced her. I tried to give her courage, so she would keep on searching. I was there and I would have defended her had the old man been there.

—Did you say "old man"?

—Yes, Mr. Ramirez. A few seconds later I discovered him. She was trying to convince me of the futility of searching any further, when . . . a few feet away . . . we heard difficult breathing . . .

—The old man.

—Yes, she muffled a cry of horror. Then we heard the old man's perverse, sarcastic chuckle. I asked him what he was doing there, why he was breaking into the woman's house, a woman who clearly wanted nothing to do with him. He answered that he wasn't exactly the intruder, and repeated his repulsive laughter. His voice seemed to come from below our heads, as if the infamous old man were seated. He had a raspy, quavering voice. Then he ordered us to follow his instructions, unless we wanted to become the target of his bullets.

—You had to leave and the girl had to stay.

—Exactly. If you asked me now why I acted the way I did, I wouldn't be able to answer. The dreadful man had hardly finished his threat when I pounced on him like a beast. We got into a savage struggle, the old man's bony hands were clawing at my face, trying to gouge my eyes. I found the hand that held the gun. We wrestled for it; it went off. His nails dug even deeper into me than before, then released me. I felt his arm go limp. She asked me if the old man was wounded. I answered that he was still sitting in his chair, dead. She came toward me slowly, her hands searched to caress my forehead. I heard her murmur thank you. Immediately, she started to go through the dead man's pockets. There she found the passport she'd been looking for, a wallet full of bills, a small silky handbag stuffed with costly jewelry. In the end she sighed deeply with relief. She explained that if she proceeded cautiously she'd soon be a woman living without fear. The next step was to leave the building without being noticed. Then I told her we didn't have a minute to waste; somebody could have heard the shooting.

—You were making a mistake. The old man wasn't dead; he was only wounded, just waiting for the right moment to reach for the gun and empty the other bullets from the cylinder.

—I hadn't realized that.

—But I did. What you must immediately do is grab the enemy by the neck and strangle him. Press. Go ahead. He had no pity on you; he tried to gouge your eyes. Now press your fingers into his flaccid, rotting skin.

—Yes, Mr. Ramirez, thanks, I'm obeying you.

—All that can be heard now is the death rattle.

—When he stopped breathing, I moved away and he fell from his chair onto the floor. "He's dead now," I told her. Then I felt her fingers on my face. My lips. And she gently pressed her own against mine. She didn't really kiss me; she just touched me very softly, with great tenderness. She said that she was leaving, and that maybe we would never see each other again.

—You asked her to take you with her, because without her you would fall back into solitude and sadness.

—No. I didn't dare.

—You did, and she didn't reply. You told her then that she was abandoning you because you were a poor bastard with nothing in this world, not even a reliable memory, a poor bastard who doesn't even know who he is.

—She touched my lips again and told me that she was going to tell me who I was. And that she loved me very much because she knew me very well.

—And then, Larry?

—Then she said that I was the man who had saved her.

—At last.

—And she took my hands, and seemed to stop thinking about leaving.

—What made you think that?

—I don't know . . . something gave me that impression.

—What? Try to remember! What gave you that impression?

—Mr. Ramirez . . . I'm trying to remember, believe me, I'm really trying . . . and it's no use. . . . I can't remember anything . . .

—But afterward! What happened?

—Mr. Ramirez . . . don't shout like that . . . in this darkness I can't see your face . . . but your shouting sounds so bad . . . it makes me think you're angry . . . furious at me . . . your bony hands are clawing at my eyes to gouge them . . .

—Me? I have only the strength to . . . to breathe . . . with difficulty . . . that frightened you . . . so much . . .

— . . .

—Larry . . . Larry . . .

— . . .

—Don't go . . . where are you? I'm awfully cold . . . Larry . . . answer me . . .

—What are you doing here?

—I heard you had been taken to the hospital, and I came to visit you.

—Is this a paid visit . . . or what?

—It doesn't matter.

—It's Wednesday, and it's two o'clock. So you should be paid.

—All right.

—I feel better now . . . but don't look at me like that.

—How?

—I must look like a ghost.

—A little pale maybe, but your voice, Mr. Ramirez? . . .

—At two o'clock you were supposed to go to the home. How come . . . you're here?

—I shouldn't be. I should still be at Columbia.

—Oh yes, you said something about that yesterday.

—Right, but I had a hunch something was wrong, so I called the home first, and they told me you were here.

—So you did not show up for your interview. Strange.

—I showed up, all right, but as far as I was concerned, I should have stayed home.

— . . .

—I didn't ask for the interview. I'd met a friend in the street, and he forced me to go see him at Columbia, where he's in a good position now. He insists I should go back to teaching.

—But you, what did you say that time? "I don't feel ready."

—Precisely. I went all the way up there because I didn't want to stand him up. But the minute a problem arose I knew that I'd been eliminated and came down here.

—You mean you've been up there already.

—Yeah, I stayed less than half an hour.

—I see . . .

— . . .

—Larry, I didn't phone them. Even if they'd asked me I wouldn't have said a thing.

—What are you talking about?

—I thought that somebody mean, somebody envious might have called the Columbia people and told them the wrong things about you.

—That's crazy. Nobody knows or cares about what I do.

—If I were mean, I could have told them about your politics.

—They would have thought you were nuts.

—But I'm not, that's why I didn't call them. My body is sick, not my mind.

—Yeah, but what you were thinking is crazy.

—I don't agree. You see, in the encyclopedia I read about birds, sparrows in particular. And how they care for their young. They build a nest, and keep the eggs warm and protected, did you know?

—Yes, that's common knowledge, one watches the nest while the other goes for food. They encourage their offspring to fly a little at a time. The offspring are fed until they can gather their own food, and eventually, when they're able to survive on their own, they're forced to leave.

—Then you'll understand me without any problem. When I was reading I thought that I would also have taken care of my son, if I had had one. Because when you see somebody smaller, you immediately know that you can do things for him that he can't. But then the son grows up, and you see he doesn't need you anymore, and you let him go. But wait . . . that's not what I was trying to say, I'm sorry, I'm lost.

—But you thought of telephoning the university, and

telling them about my left-wing politics so that I wouldn't get the job. That's hardly protective behavior. You're hostile toward me, but I've done nothing to you. I can barely eke out a living.

—Did you have lunch at that restaurant you like?

—No, I went back home; I had a sandwich.

—Why? I left you an envelope with money at the home.

—When I passed by last night the offices were closed. Anyway, I don't want you to leave me anything anymore.

—Why?

—I don't like to owe favors. If you should ever ask me for something, I want to be able to say no if I feel like it.

—You went back home to feed your cat. . . . Your cat would have liked one of those tender young sparrows I told you about. You would have liked to give your cat one of those birds, but the ones in the encyclopedia are made out of paper.

—I don't have my cat anymore.

—What happened?

—Sometimes people lie for no reason. I used to have a cat, but it died months ago. I don't know why I told you I still had it.

—Don't you think this room is comfortable? They can raise and lower the bed. And this buzzer, I like it best of all. Should a stranger come in I can call an attendant, who'd rid me of him immediately. There's no such facility at the home.

—So what happened? Why are you feeling worse?

—My blood pressure dropped. My blood-sugar level's too high. If things continue like this I won't live very long, it seems.

—You're depressed. And envious of people around you. You turn them into enemies.

—Strange that you would say that. At times when I was depressed you never acknowledged it, and now that I'm not you tell me I am. I have no reason to be depressed. You're here and I have somebody to talk to. When you leave I will have nobody, then maybe yes, I'll get depressed, but that won't last very long if I get a good book to read. The one who has reason to be depressed is you, because you wasted your morning uptown.

— . . .

—But if you think so, you're a fool, I'd change places with you anytime . . . I thought of you last night, when they brought me here. The room at the home was vacant and there was no need for you to spend the night on the E train. But I had no way of reaching you. Even if I had had a number where I could reach you, I was so sick I couldn't have dialed it. When they first brought me here they took me to Intensive Care. I was in an oxygen tent until this morning . . .

—It's all right, Mr. Ramirez. I'm fine; when you get better we can go out again. The weather is getting nicer.

— . . .

—What's this package? It's addressed to you, Mr. Ramirez.

—Yes, a messenger from the committee brought it this morning. But I won't open it. They made a mistake. It's not for me.

—What can it be? The sender is a human rights organization in Buenos Aires.

—Now . . . I know what I wanted to say . . . before. The sparrows, and all kind of birds . . . and maybe all animals, they take care of their young . . . while they are . . . small . . . in size. When the offspring grow, their parents no longer know . . . who they are . . . they don't recognize their children anymore . . . because they have no memory, the way people do.

—It's a blessing.

—No . . . not at all. . . . Since I came to this city . . . and started to feel better . . . when I started to read . . . well, you know . . . you understand. . . . Today, if a son of mine were lying in the street, bleeding . . . I would recognize him . . . I would try to help him . . . because I can remember things . . . I recognize you each day you come . . . but not before . . . before they put me on the plane . . . I wouldn't have recognized my son . . . just like the animals. . . . So . . . you said I was going to call the university . . . and tell them about you . . . but I thought of that . . . because when somebody has your . . . ideas . . . he must watch out . . . it was not I who was going to make the phone call . . . but some enemy of yours . . . or a false friend . . .

—So you're my friend?

—That's not like you; you seldom ask questions. What is it, Larry? Don't you recognize me . . . anymore?

—Who are you?

—Sometimes . . . people . . . have to take chances, Larry . . . I know you're just a boy . . . but you must think you're big and strong . . . because I'm going to need help . . . and you're the only one around . . .

— . . .

—You must not tell anybody . . . first of all, don't tell your mother. . . . But today . . . it has happened to me again . . . I don't remember anything. . . . Are you going to help me?

—Yeah, I'll help you.

—Little boy . . . I must go to work . . . I must go and bring your mother some money for the house. . . . She'll be very upset if there's nothing to eat tonight . . . but I don't remember anything. . . . Where do I work? . . . How do I get there? . . . You must tell me what I have to do . . .

—Take the bus.

—But I can't go like this. . . . Should I shave? . . . What should I wear? . . . Is it an elegant office where I'm going? . . . Please help me . . .

—Shave and put on a suit.

—My best suit?

—Any suit will do.

—Why don't you help me? . . . Tell me . . . please . . . everything . . . it's getting late . . .

—What do you want to know?

—All that I have to do to please your mother and you.

—Even if you do everything, it's expected of you. We won't be pleased.

—Ah . . . ah . . .

—What is it? You can't breathe?

—Because you're too little . . . and you . . . cannot help me . . .

—I don't like the way . . . you force me to do things for you . . . but, first you have to get up very early, before the sun comes up, though you'll still need to sleep two or three hours more. The alarm goes off; it's jarring . . . and rude, crashing into your dreams . . . and feelings. Some asshole's already hollering on the radio. Your eyelids feel like weights . . . your back is heavy . . . and clings to the mattress . . . but you manage to sit up in bed, and open your eyes . . . and interrupt your dreams . . . to pay attention to . . . the clock, use the bathroom, the toothbrush . . . have breakfast, make time. . . . You look at yourself in the mirror; you get dressed; you gulp down food; you run to the bus. . . . Your resentment builds because you have to do this; you're cranky and irritable. And the day begins at the factory. . . . Matters are urgent.

—What is my job?

—You still want to go to work?

—You must forgive me . . . of course, I know you want to play with me . . . you want to go fly your kite . . . play ball . . . with me. But that is impossible; one day you'll realize why . . . so now be good and tell me how to do my job . . .

—I'm still sleeping when you leave for work. Sometimes you stop in my room, pat me on the head . . .

—With one hand? . . . Or both? . . .

—One.

—And then?

—You leave for work.

—Do I gasp? . . . Am I breathless because I have to leave for work?

—No.

—I think I remember losing my breath . . . once . . . or even more than once . . . but you have forgotten.

—Yes, I don't remember, I'm always asleep before you leave.

—Do I shout at work?

—No, never. Your job is not important. When you die they'll find a younger man to replace you, and they'll break him in . . . in a few weeks.

—I won't die; not before you grow up and can provide for yourself.

—What a good father you are. . . . Father.

—Are you laughing at me? It's hardly the right moment; I'll be late for my job. And you're wrong, they would never think of replacing me.

—The boss will love you. And make sure you go to church on Sunday. That way you will be penned in on three sides. Family, job, religion. Ideal citizen. Egyptian fellah, faceless man. The neighbors will say what a good husband you are.

—Yes, but you don't seem to like that; you're laughing at all of it. If I go to work and obey orders it's because you and your mother and myself, we all have to eat. I'm so afraid they'll discover my real values and fire me.

—Once you were laid off at the factory where you had worked as a foreman for years. And you had to take a horrible job. In another factory. Working a die-cut press.

—I can't operate it, I have forgotten how. Maybe tomorrow everything will come back to me. But what about today? I can't go to that factory today.

—A die-cut press is not difficult to operate. You just have to be fast, and be able to stand the noise. And the exhaustion. And the mindlessness. That's all. The job itself is simple.

—Could you teach me?

—All right. You know what a die is?

—No.

—It's a heavy piece of metal, shaped like . . . like an envelope, for example, with sharp edges. You put a ream of paper on the press, then you put the die on top of it. Then a heavy weight comes crashing down on the die and cuts the paper. You take the die off; take out and stack the paper; put in another ream; put the die back on before the weight comes crashing down again. The press is mechanized for a quota, and you must move fast enough to keep up with it. If the die is not placed right . . . it can shoot out and hurt you. You must move quickly and precisely.

—Wait, let me see if I can do it . . . I put the paper . . . I put the die on . . . and the weight? How does it come down?

—On your hands, if you're not careful.

—I'll be careful.

—The press is automatic; it's timed. The boss times it.

—I understand now. If I don't take my hands off, they will be smashed.

—Yes. Although the job's mindless, you must be alert at all times.

—Very well . . . but . . . let's see . . . the crash comes down . . . I'll have taken my hands off before . . . I'll be paying attention . . . but what's next?

—You remove the die.

—The die.

—You take out the cut paper. Stack it on the right.

—Stack it on the right.

—Grab a new ream of paper from your left. Stack it evenly on the press.

—...

—Put the die back on, and remove your hands.

—Yes, thanks; I know why, because the weight is timed and will come down. And then I take out the cut paper ... but ... I don't know where to stack it.

—Stack it on your right.

—Yes, it's all coming back to me. And I'll stay alert, and even if I get tired I won't let the boss notice.

—He doesn't care if you look tired; if you are tired; if you're ready to faint; as long as you keep working.

—I won't faint, I promise. But will it ever stop? Will I know when I'm allowed to stop?

—You get a fifteen-minute coffee break in the morning and in the afternoon. At lunchtime you'll be happy to get out of there, to breathe fresh air, to look at the sky, to see colors. To order what you want to eat. To eat a lot. To smoke a cigarette. To choose what block you want to walk down, to say a few words to somebody. But soon it will be time to go back. And the machines will start up again. There are lots of presses in the shop, and the din will be deafening.

—You're afraid I'll feel sick inside there, but I won't. This place may be awful, but if I know I'll be let out, I'll put up with it. And I know that in the evening I'll be able to go home.

—You may bum around the city for an hour. To spend less time with your wife.

—No, I was afraid you and your mother would think that. If I arrive late today it's because I was shopping for a present.

—You're such a good father.

—Again you don't want to believe me, or be pleased with what I say.

—Nobody in a family is ever pleased with another member. Even if everyone plays his or her role perfectly. That's part of what a family is about, Mr. Ramirez.

—You are only saying that so I won't worry about letting you down. I know you expect a lot from me, and I won't disappoint you.

—Are you sure you don't want to open this package?

—It's not for me.

—Who is it for?

—Somebody else. Throw it in the garbage.

—First, let's see what it is.

—Do whatever you want, as long as you don't show it to me.

—Let's open it.

—You should wait until your mother comes to the table . . . to unwrap it.

—To hell with her.

—Maybe I'm wrong, but I thought you had to wait for Christmas to unwrap presents . . . or for birthdays. That was one of the first things I read when I came to the home . . . it was in a novel. . . . The father arrived with presents for the family . . . but again, you see . . . I made a note of it, but I left it at the home.

—There's a bunch of French novels in this package. Elegant editions . . .

—For whom could this present be?

—*Les Liaisons Dangereuses, La Princesse de Cleves, Adolphe,* beautiful . . . were you into this stuff?

—They are not for me . . .

—Sure they are . . . they're probably your own books. Sure, your name is in all of them. And the dates . . . 1928 . . . 1930. No wonder the paper has turned brown . . .

— . . .

—What are these numbers?

— . . .

—What are these numbers above the words? They seem random. 32, 1, 3, 16, 5, 12, 4 . . .

— . . .

—Hmm . . . if you rearrange the numbered words sequentially they form sentences.

—Nonsense. Some child must have scribbled those numbers, that's all . . .

—No . . . it does . . . look.

—Well, be reasonable . . . I've been working all day; I can't start playing with you the very minute I get home . . .

—I think these are the notes you made while you were in prison. Very clever!

—Little boy . . . when are you going to grow up?

—Mr. Ramirez, you had a lot of guts. The numbers are in your handwriting.

— . . .

—This could be important. Let me write it out. "Malédiction eternelle . . . à . . . qui . . . lise . . . ces pages"—That's the first thing it says. "Eternal curse on the reader of these pages."

—I told you to throw the package in the garbage.

—No, let's see what you were up to. You seem to be discussing a general strike . . . on some pages you found a lot of words you could use . . . on others not so many . . .

— . . .

—This page is in letter form . . . you used the same introduction as the character. This whole novel is composed of letters, as you may remember.

—There are no novels in French at the home.

—Eternal curse on whom? On the policeman who'd open this book and read these pages?

— . . .

—Eternal curse on whomever reads it with evil eyes, with policemen's eyes?

—Policemen help people, they stop the traffic when someone in a wheelchair has to cross the street.

—Mr. Ramirez, you know I'm not an informer. Why are you so cautious with me?

— . . .

—This could be important. I want to write this out. . . . It could be an important document about resistance to repression.

—It's not.

—May I keep these books for a few days?

—You seem so happy . . . what has made you so excited?

—It may be material I could use . . . write about . . .

—These old books make you happy? . . . I don't know why I chose them . . . I must have known they were the ones you wanted . . . as a present . . . I don't even remember where I got them . . .

—Yes, they're just what I wanted . . . thanks very much . . .

—I'm so relieved . . . I wasn't sure you were going to like them . . . I told myself, his last birthday was such a happy occasion . . . it will be difficult not to disappoint him this time . . .

—No, they're beautiful, perfect . . .

—Now . . . may I be frank? I know your last birthday was a wonderful day . . . but I don't remember any of the details . . . so, in order for me to surpass it today . . . you must tell me everything that happened . . .

—Sickening . . . it's a sickening subject . . .

—Larry, I don't understand . . .

—Little kids have birthday parties . . . when they are five or six . . .

—If you don't tell me what I want to know, I'll take those books away from you.

—You're going to get out of bed and fight me?

—I'm listening . . .

—All right . . . you could invite all your little friends on the block, whomever you wanted . . . you had a choice. For that day, or for those few hours, you were king. I remember inviting lots of little girls and only a few boys. There was always a big cake, lots of candy. And presents for everybody. All the kids who were invited had to bring a present. And it was great fun opening up ten presents or so.

—Which ones did you like best?

—The only thing I didn't like were those little cone-shaped caps with the rubber band that went under your chin.

—Why not?

—They made me look like an idiot. Wearing one was like having your prick sticking out of your head. I hated them. And you know I still never wear hats.

—Your prick sticking out of your head?

—Those caps made me feel humiliated. But my mother would force me to wear them. You know, I didn't go to my college graduation because I would have had to have worn . . . a hat. Hats are ugly. Cone-shaped ones at birthday and New Year's Eve parties, square ones at graduations, baseball caps with peaks; something that shouldn't be there sticks out of them. Something funny-looking.

—Larry, I don't know. . . . Does a little boy have a big penis? Or does it grow while he grows?

—It's enormous. And unruly. An embarrassment. Very different from the rest of the body. Strange and ugly, hanging . . . from the body. Hidden most of the time. Something to be ashamed of.

—You mean then . . . that little boys . . . can be as effective with a woman . . . as men? . . .

—That's a good question. Little boys definitely have erections. And perhaps should be encouraged to try it.

—No . . . you're lying to me. . . . Now I remember the young boys in the encyclopedia. They had tiny penises, and no pubic hair . . . like angels in church paintings.

—One's feelings are mixed . . . regarding this object. On the one hand, you're proud of it, you wouldn't like anything to happen to it. On the other, it's embarrassing; it acts up on its own. It must already have been paradoxical at the time . . .

—At what time?

—At the age of five . . . I then had to suppress desire. I guess the fact that my mother forced me to wear cone-shaped caps . . . and even put them on . . . for me . . . made it more unbearable. Though it is probably exactly what I would have wished . . . for her to fondle me . . .

—To fondle your tiny penis?

—It ain't all that tiny. And a child feels that his desires are as strong as his father's. The father is there . . . merely by virtue of his bigness. But in no other way is he superior.

—But that was the happiest birthday you've had, until this one today. So you must tell me what happened after your mother put the rubber string of the cone-shaped hat under your chin.

—I don't have to tell you anything, you parasite.

—You're afraid I'll tell her.

—It's unjust. The father's position. That the accidental and temporary condition of his larger size . . . should give him exclusive rights to the mother. My mother wanted me also, I know it. But I couldn't have done as good a job at that time as my father. It's painful to admit that because of your goddamn frame . . . you can't have the woman. And it's hard to give her up, even now . . . the longing remains . . .

—Given the least encouragement you repeat that nonsense. Somebody told you that and you believed him.

—It's true, the longing remains.

—Somebody invented that story and you believed him. You're afraid that if that . . . longing doesn't exist, there won't be anything to replace it. That's why you believed the foolishness they told you. Maybe, like me, you are most afraid of not remembering what was there instead of that false desire, that senseless lie.

— . . .

—Larry, later on . . . when she arrives . . . I'm not sure of something . . . has it been a long time since you last saw her?

— . . .

—Well, you may not like it . . . but . . . she's not the same. . . . So . . . when she sees you . . . who knows what her reaction will be . . . and it's not that she's like an animal . . . like those sparrows, so primitive they can't recognize their own offspring . . . once they grow up. . . . In this case the reasons would be different . . .

—What reasons?

—Not so loud . . . she must not hear you. Don't let her know that we find her so changed. She could be hurt. Let's pretend everything is as it used to be.

— . . .

—She's standing there, Larry. Maybe she's waiting for me to say something. What should one tell her?

—Go talk to her. Ask her how she's been.

—She tells me she's feeling well but doesn't know why. Let's not tell her right away. Maybe she will realize it's the anniversary of her giving birth to you.

— . . .

—I'll tell her only that you're a young man, visiting; that it is your birthday; and that there are things you like and things you don't. That she shouldn't do anything she used to do to her children, like force you to wear those hats. All she has to do is check with you first.

—Has she been ill? Is she sick?

—No . . . she looks so well, so youthful; why do you think she's been ill?

—You've already said she's not the same as before.

—That's the only thing one shouldn't mention to her.

—Really?

—Maybe there's something else she would prefer not to discuss, Larry. I'm sure that she, like myself, doesn't want to think about what happened . . . long ago.

—But it's killing you. It's too costly not to recall.

—You must not forget I worked all day . . . and what's more . . . today is a special occasion, a day we're going to remember forever, a great reunion. All problems should be put aside . . . until tomorrow.

— . . .

—I see that she doesn't dare do anything, even take a step . . . in any direction. Maybe you, Larry, should come closer and whisper to her what to do, without anybody noticing. I know well what it's like; sometimes the slightest hint would help me find my way. People don't notice; they believe I'm self-assured.

—Good idea.

—You're the only one . . . in this warm, elegant drawing room . . . who knows what needs to be done.

—Go introduce yourself, Mr. Ramirez. Then you can introduce me.

—Well . . . it's done . . . in a way, because she has realized by now that you're the one who has all the answers . . . and please . . . don't let her notice that she's already made one mistake.

—If I have all the answers then I'm the head of the family, her husband.

—This has to be the happiest of occasions. So we must go to great pains to make it so . . .

—You want me to be her husband?

—Why do you say that? You're the only one who can give her and me proper instructions . . . and you'll see, toward the end of the evening, if you've been helpful and clear enough, she will be able to answer all your questions about the son.

—What about the husband? Mr. Ramirez, she should be more interested in him than in the son.

—All right . . . just by a whisper . . . help her . . . tell her what she must know about her husband. . . . But tell her the truth. . . . Or maybe not; tell her what she'd like to hear

. . . because if you tell her that he was exactly as she'd like him to be, if you help her, then he . . . may . . .

—May what, Mr. Ramirez?

—May agree.

—Agree on what?

—He might listen and behave as he should.

—Yes, but what do you mean by that? What would happen later?

— . . .

—The father puts a heavy burden on the children; to occupy the mother's attention and please her. He probably agreed to have three children, so as to pacify her, hoping she'll be preoccupied with them, and make fewer demands on him.

—Larry, please . . . tell her . . . what demands shouldn't she make? . . .

—It's not that she shouldn't make those demands on him, but that he feels he can't cope with them.

—Please . . . tell him . . . how he could meet those demands . . .

—It's not easy. She's not satisfied with her role as a married woman, a housewife, a mother . . . it was not what she had expected. It's hard, and they're poor. Father works long hours, and spends little time with her.

—Don't remind her of all that. Let's save time. Tell him what he should do today, to make it the happiest occasion ever.

—He should spend time with her. Talk to her. It doesn't matter on what subject. He should take her out someplace, to a restaurant, dancing, a movie.

—But you told me they are poor.

—Yes, but it's very important to do what I've said, to find a way.

—But she's just arrived, and it's their son's birthday . . . and he's a young man . . . and he's waiting for his father to say something . . . to do something that will make this . . . the happiest day ever . . . for his wife and his son . . .

—. . .

—. . .

—They had very little time together . . . Mr. Ramirez. She complains about her problems to him. He complains about his to her. They're tired. What remains between them is very little. And it must make magic again. But he doesn't take her out. He doesn't like crowds . . . or parties. He's socially inept.

—I told you not to remind her of those things. . . . Luckily she couldn't hear you . . . she's fallen asleep . . . and I'm so tired, too . . . I'm going to lie here on the sofa, next to her . . .

—Why not in the bedroom?

—No, Larry, not there.

—Should I lift her up and take her to the bedroom?

—No!

—Why not?

—You've already done all you could to help us on this day. You may retire.

—Won't you allow me to do anything else?

—You're Larry; you work here. You should be content with that, with knowing exactly what your chores are. You've done your job for today, and now you can go and look after your cat. It may still be alive. I don't know when you're lying to me and when you're not.

—The cat has disappeared; I took for granted that it was dead. But it may reappear at any moment.

—Don't look at her like that. I know what's going through your mind. That she's like one of those birds. But it isn't true. Tomorrow she'll wake up and feel better, and everything will change.

—How?

—She needs good care; she needs help. And when she feels out of danger . . .

—The cat better not come back then.

—Why?

—Haven't you ever seen a cat catch a bird and swallow it whole?

—Shut up! . . . Why do you want to frighten her? Had she heard you she wouldn't have been able to sleep all night . . .

—That was my intention, Mr. Ramirez.

—I'll keep watch over her all night long then. I won't let anything happen to her. So when she wakes up in the morning everything will change.

—There we go again. Nothing will change.

—Yes, because I'm going to ask her a question and she's going to answer.

—What?

—If I could I'd keep watch over her all night; she could be attacked, Larry.

—By the cat?

—Don't be a nuisance. She's going to be very grateful and won't know how to repay me. One of the things she'll say is that I saved her by seeing her through a critical trance. Then she'll grab my hands and won't feel like leaving anymore.

—What makes you think she won't?

—Tonight I didn't let her know I didn't remember who I am. I didn't ask her anything. I was wrong; maybe she knew anyhow; I shouldn't have been ashamed. I didn't want to disturb her, I let her sleep peacefully . . . because there was nothing else to fear.

—Do you think so?

—There's nothing else to fear because I'll defend her even if it costs me my life. But I do admit that I should have asked her.

—What?

—I should have asked who I am. But I got frightened. There's nothing I fear more . . . than her reply.

—Are you sure?

—My eyes are closing, too; I'm so sleepy. . . . Although I should keep watch over her. You know something? Today I received a present . . . and I'd like to sleep holding it. . . . Would you mind handing me those books? . . . They are mine . . . I got them as a present . . .

— . . .

—Why are you so surprised? Aren't you going to give them back to me?

—Sure. . . . Here they are . . .

—Tomorrow . . . if you want . . . to take another look at them . . . you may come back . . . and I'll willingly lend them to you. . . . But just to look at them here . . . if you take them outside they could get lost, or something even worse could happen . . .

Part Two

—Am I disturbing you?

—Oh . . . no. . . . Is it you, Larry?

—Yes.

—Come in . . .

—Why is it so dark in here? Do you want some light?

—As you wish . . . you may draw the curtains, go ahead . . .

—Great . . . it's like a tomb in here . . . well, a hospital is halfway there.

—It's Saturday, isn't it? So why have you come?

—I came to work on the books a bit.

—Oh . . . it's a pity we can't go out today. It looks sunny and is not too cold.

—You want to go out . . . I'll take you out . . .

—You must be joking. My condition hasn't improved, you know?

—Fresh air will do you good.

—The doctor said I shouldn't be surprised if they take me again into Intensive Care. That's how improved he found me. . . . They were worrying about my losing my eyesight. . . . It happened this morning . . . I thought it was a cloudy day . . . and the male nurse . . . when he came in . . . I thought he was you.

—What's wrong with your eyes?

—I can see only your outline clearly . . . not your face.

—Where did you put the books?

—When you opened the curtains I appreciated the difference in light. But not seeing too well makes me a little sleepy. . . . It would be great to talk to you for a while . . . soon I'll fall asleep and you'll be able to read all you want.

—O.K., just tell me where the books are before you fall asleep.

—Oh . . . don't worry . . . I'll give them to you. You see . . . this will certainly be the only chance I'll get . . . to talk to someone . . . all day.

—Don't think I'm going to talk to anybody else either.

—Is that so?

—Since the day I went to Columbia I haven't talked to a soul but you, period.

—Why?

—I don't like chit-chat. Anyway, who would want to talk to me?

—Anyone! You might seem healthy and full of life.

—I *am* healthy and full of life.

—But . . . don't think that I need to talk to just anyone. Certainly not to shrinks, as you call them. If there's something I like about being here at the hospital . . . it's not seeing them.

—They only try to help.

—But they don't succeed. I prefer to read . . . although I must admit . . . when I'm able to see you I understand better what you're trying to say.

—But you keep getting sicker.

—The male nurse said the same thing to me this morning. He used exactly the same words. Sometimes I'm afraid people are joking at my expense . . . getting me confused . . . making me believe they are not who they are. Is it really you or the male nurse who's talking? I don't trust him.

— . . .

—If you don't talk I can't be sure it's you, Larry, who's come to see me.

—Who else would?

—You never said anything about the gangs.

—What gangs?

—If it hadn't been for the paper, I wouldn't have found out. I could have gone out in the street . . . unarmed.

—I just bit my lip and you did the same. Your vision can't be that bad.

—What . . . Larry?

—I bit my lip and you repeated the same gesture, like a monkey.

—Why didn't you tell me about the gangs in the streets? They must be frightening.

—What are you talking about?

—They're very young, but violent, dangerous. The male nurse brought me the evening paper because I couldn't go to sleep last night. You must tell me how to protect myself.

—I won't tell you shit. I wish you'd stop telling me I must do this or that. It's irritating.

— . . .

—Tell me where you put those books.

—I'm terribly frightened by the gangs. The article in the paper was full of details. I read that . . . and then something on the new Catholic church . . . anything to forget about the gangs.

—Let me work on the books. It's more important than this conversation. Something productive may come from them.

—You sound angry. I wonder how your face looks now.

—Your blindness is fake; you can see.

—Last night I woke up with the fear . . . that today somebody would come up . . . and ask me for the books. By now . . . they may know the books have arrived . . . and just today it had to happen; my eyesight had to fail me . . .

—I'm not Larry today. Do you want another friend?

—No . . . and the books . . . you'll never be able to find . . .

—Shove your books.

—That's not polite . . . to say the least.

—You're impolite. Worse than impolite . . . you're manipulative and scheming. I don't like it . . . I won't be blackmailed . . . the books are not so important to me that I'll put up with this shit . . . to get them. If you don't want me to work on them, just say so.

—Manipulative? Scheming? Isn't all that a little beyond my reach? I haven't got the power to manipulate . . .

—You have plenty of energy . . . you must have been a terror on your feet.

—There's no proof of that . . . none at all. There will never be.

— . . .

—Why won't you talk to me?

—Where did you read about the gangs?

—In the evening paper.

—What did it say?

—You must know; you are a native of this town. Horrible youth gangs loose in the streets.

—For me it wasn't like that at all. You know, a working-class neighborhood is like the barracks. People go to work; they come home. They're tired, and they sleep. Watch television. Wash the car. Mow the lawn. Go to church. It's oppressive. There was nothing for young people to do. Life was organized around work and recuperation. And work didn't take place in the neighborhood itself. So there was nothing there, a vacuum. The kids were extremely bored, but they created their own reality . . . in gangs.

—Beating up people? Killing each other?

—Not really. There was more talk than action . . . talk about physical prowess and fights . . . which occasionally were staged to sustain the reality of the gang. We met on street corners late at night; smoked cigarettes; drank beer; rode around in cars; went to movies and bowling alleys; made a lot of noise; and looked for adventure.

—Adventure . . .

—Some excitement, something new. Something risky . . .

—Robbing, raping, killing people?

—We never went that far. We liked to upset conventional standards. Provoke some reaction from boring adults. Do anything to show we were different.

—Can you remember a rule you broke?

—One night we stole a bus from a gas station, and drove it to the beach. It was very exciting. The keys had been left in the bus, and we pried the door open. We had the tallest and oldest-looking guy drive the thing. He had to comb his hair in a different way, so as not to look like a teenager. The rest of us pretended we were passengers, staring out the windows, with glazed expressions. We found some hats to wear, newspapers. After passing patrol cars on the road, we howled and screamed with delight. We drove to the beach, swam and drove back, parking the bus in the same space at the gas station. But turned around the other way. We talked about that night for years.

—You're not afraid of gangs, then.

—Not really.

—You're brave. Now, you see, I'm not afraid either because you have given me sufficient proof of your identity.

—Like what?

—Last night the intern offered to get a priest to come see me. I refused his offer. Have you known any priests?

—Yeah, a few. What about them?

—I don't trust them. Could you tell me something about them?

—Could we talk about something more pleasant? Sports, anything else?

—Don't joke around. One of these nights I may lose consciousness and they'll come and absolve me.

—Do they charge for the service?

—You dislike them so strongly. Tell me what they did to you.

—I'm not interested in the subject. It's such an obvious anachronism—and reactionary. So easy to take potshots at. Like beating a dead horse. But the horse isn't dead.

—You said your father was a good worker and went to church, too.

—My father never went to church. He was a true pagan.

One of his strong points. His indifference to religion, I liked that about him. But he was indifferent to politics, too. He felt it was all bullshit, because neither religion nor politics impinged on his life.

—Never mind, Larry. . . . By the way, here is the key.

—To what?

—To that locker over there, the books are inside. Keep the key, but don't lose it.

—I won't.

—So . . . maybe if you continue to tell me things I'll recall more . . . not only my first years but my first excursions as well . . .

—I see.

—Encounters . . . happy encounters, I'm sure there were some.

—Maybe.

—Wouldn't you like to tell me the good things that can happen to a young man?

—I remember when I first started reading, what a joy that was. It was around puberty, I had read before, of course, in school, textbooks. But it was always a drag. In grammar school they used to make us go to the library once a week, force us to choose a book, sit down and read it for an hour. And then give a report on it the next day. We all hated the library. I remember they had a whole series of skinny little books on Central America, one for each country, Costa Rica, Honduras, Panama. . . . They were pretty, and had lots of color pictures, but I never liked reading the text. That all changed with puberty. I devoured books after school. That was my religious phase.

—Who told you to read?

—No one; I'd just pick books up. In the church there were books. The Bible, the Book of Common Prayer. The priests used to read from them.

—Did they read aloud to you?

—Yes, at mass. I was an altar boy. And sometimes I would

serve at the early weekday morning mass, when no one was
there but the priest and myself. He was a gigantic beefy
man, with a face like raw steak. He had steel-rimmed glasses.
He wore a red skirt and a white doily wrapped around him.
He had crew-cut gray hair.

—Like yours.

—Maybe. Mass was at six o'clock. I had to get up very
early and walk about a mile to the church. Sometimes it was
cold, and a little dark, but I loved it, because the priest and
I were there alone. No one ever came to those masses.
Sometimes he was tired and cranky and had bad breath. He
would race through some of the prayers, and I had to say
"Amen," "Amen," "Amen" . . . but afterward was best. We
would have breakfast in the rectory. Then he was relaxed
and happy. He used to buy more expensive bread than my
mother, and it made the most delicious toast. We would
listen to the news on the radio, and he would talk to me. I
would then go to school.

—Do you by chance remember what he used to say?

—He would ask me what I was doing in school. And he
would actually ask my opinion about things, as if I were a
little man. That pleased me very much.

—Did he recommend any books to you?

—I don't remember. But he had a big library. And I was
always borrowing this and that.

—Picture books? Novels? Poetry?

—No, big history books and religious books.

—Were you sorry that you had to give them back?

—No, I could always borrow others. Once he gave me a
present, a little black book with gold printing, containing
excerpts from Saint Augustine. I read it a thousand times.
The book never made any sense to me, but I convinced
myself that I enjoyed it.

— . . .

—Then I started reading things on my own. Philosophy,
theology, the more complicated the better. I especially loved

long convoluted sentences, with phrases harking back to other phrases. The subject was not important; it was the movement of the sentences, their logic, their beauty, their complicated architecture that gave me pleasure. I guess what was coming alive at that time was my capacity for pleasure. But my mother would throw out all my books. There is a chapter in Sartre's *Being and Nothingness* called "The Body." She thought the book was pornographic and threw it out. What she didn't understand and what gave me pleasure were suspicious to her.

—Did your father think it was pornographic?

—My father could barely read the *Daily News.* And my mother used to berate him for his illiteracy.

—Who gave you the money to buy books?

—I got an allowance that I saved up. And I was the treasurer of the Altar Boys' Club. I used to dip into their funds once in awhile. Sometimes I would steal money that was lying around the house. And you could always get secondhand books cheap.

—Did someone tell you what to read?

—No, I read what I felt like reading. Chose my own topics. I felt that I was entering a limitless world of unending adventures.

—When I read I recognize the words, but I don't believe some of them.

— . . .

—Won't you ask me which ones? Why don't you ask me questions?

—I was searching for a vocabulary to name all I was discovering. Religion gave me my first vocabulary. I was so religious at that time. Until evil thoughts started breaking through, raw, undisguised.

—Evil thoughts?

—My whole religious framework collapsed. I felt I was giving up my morality.

—Did you find somebody to discuss those books with?

—No. My buddies didn't read and thought I was eccentric, thought I was an egghead. That term had currency in those days. It came out of McCarthy era. A derogatory word for intellectuals.

—One day we were in front of the tree, the old one in the park I liked so much. But I didn't feel like touching it. The tree was there, and I could look at it whenever I wanted. There was no reason to touch it; it wasn't going to just leave and disappear forever.

—Why bring that up?

—Go on.

—I remember the first time I was infatuated—what a word!—with a girl. It was so strong. Her name was Dorman, like the cheese. She sat across the room in high-school English class. She had long curly hair, and was very sweet. Something about her grabbed me, and I would watch her during class, but still listening to what the teacher was saying because I was a good student. I would find any excuse to talk to her . . . in the hallways, anywhere. I kept losing homework assignments, and calling her up. Just hearing her say the most matter-of-fact things was a great source of pleasure to me. Her smile would melt me. She was in reality how I've described her—very sweet—but one attributes many virtues to the person one is infatuated with.

—Why?

—That's a difficult question.

—So . . .

—Especially with first love, which was like a shattering of boundaries. All that had been . . . pent-up, latent, was about to reveal itself. A backlog of needs that no single person could satisfy. So the person that one is infatuated with is idealized, in the hope that she will satisfy all one's needs.

—Needs?

—Yeah, needs.

—What are they?

—It's hard to say what they are. First I thought they were religious. Then intellectual. Then I thought they had to do with girls. It's energy mostly, energy that explodes at puberty. A time bomb in the body . . .

—Would you be so kind as to tell me, in order, what are . . . or were, religious needs. Then the intellectual ones. Maybe I can guess what it was like regarding girls. I just thought of my need for sweets, and since you described that young girl as sweet, I made the connection. Does that make any sense?

—Yes, it's like the need for sweets. Very much so. It's something the body craves, something you feel you could never devour enough of. You become a glutton. Insatiable. You can't stop feeling like you're missing something.

—What's the missing part?

—It's nothing specific. But you feel you have a gaping wound, that you can't do anything else until you're healed, until you're satisfied. It's very much like hunger, you understand.

—Then religious needs are not like hunger.

—At puberty they were. I was voracious. But all that ended at thirteen. Certain images were transfigured.

—Tell me about one of those images?

—No, I can't.

—Which was first?

—I don't know. God and Christ as men, Mr. Ramirez.

—What did you feel for them?

—Love and admiration. And the hour came when I wanted to transfer my feelings to a real person. An actual body with hair and with all its imperfections, a woman, a substitute for ethereal beings in white robes. Children can picture deities only in human terms, and their relation to God is always a relation to a man, a powerful man.

—A young man?

—No, an old man, powerful but loving, with whom one ingratiates oneself . . . by self-denial, self-effacement, by struggling against one's impulses. Religion services repression; but one expects to be rewarded for one's sacrifice, by a version of that which was repressed.

—I've seen religious paintings in books, and I like the children, the angels, and Christ on the cross a little, but not when he's standing. I like the women only when they're crying because Christ is carrying the cross or has been nailed to it.

—How about those sexy medieval paintings in which Mary is breast-feeding Jesus? Do you like them?

—I haven't seen them recently.

—I like them. Especially the smile of contentment on the mother's face. That's something we men will never know.

—Did you want to be an angel when you were a child? Or Jesus crucified, the center of all attention?

—At first just an angel, then a special person—singled out by Jesus for his goodness; then I wanted to supplant or become Jesus himself . . . through selflessness and suffering. But then I would be God's, and he and all the world would look on me with favor. By suffering so well, so patiently, so selflessly, I would attain God's protection and admiration.

—What does God tell his son?

— . . .

—What do they do all day long?

— . . .

—You just said "God's protection." What did you mean by that?

—That he would not get angry with or punish me. Like the Mafia; that kind of protection. Like my father.

—You mentioned God's admiration, too. What was it like?

—I hoped that he would look benevolently on me. And allow me to be, not destroy me. That he'd restrain himself. Permit me to gain the admiration of everyone. To willingly undergo punishment and suffering is like saying, "Please, Father, don't hit me, see how I hit and punish myself."

—When I asked what his protection would be like you said simply "not get angry." Then I asked about his admiration and you said "not destroy me." If the dictionary is correct, you are not . . . when you use those words.

—I did say "look down benevolently on me." But you're right, the admiration business is vague, protection is what's most important. Protection from God's power. Like the Mafia.

—What does God tell his son?

—You know, it's funny, I never imagined being God himself. Having a son to boss around.

—Try it, go ahead. Imagine one day in their life.

—A day in the life of God and his son?

—Yes.

—Where do you get your ideas?

—Do they get up early in the morning?

—Generally at six-fifteen, Mr. Ramirez.

—It's six-fifteen, the day starts.

— . . .

—What is the weather like?

—It's a great day, Mr. Ramirez. . . . Get up, kid. Want some coffee?

— . . .

—The kid's a little sleepy. Wants to sleep some more; turns over. The father shakes him by the shoulders, gruffly. Starts talking loudly. Forces him to get up. Makes him take a cold shower. And eat a big breakfast. Forces him to start the day.

—What's served at the table?

—Hearty stuff. Cereal, bread, fruits . . . and juices. No

cake. . . . The father is aggressive, outgoing, confident, no self-doubts, no hypersensitivity. Expansive.

—How is he dressed?

—Simply, in pants and a shirt. . . . The son is timid. He sees three or four sides to every question; he hesitates.

—He's prudent, then.

—So it seems. But not really. His defensiveness results in increased sensitivity. He doesn't like his father's self-assurance and cockiness. He thinks life is more complex, more subtle, richer, and, secretly, he criticizes his father as a klutz, a boor, a one-dimensional character. Simply concerned with power, and not examining any other aspect of his own life or of others'. The son rejects his father's goals and values, and secretly feels superior. But can't act. Can't decide.

—How will God demonstrate to his son that there's been a misunderstanding?

—What misunderstanding?

—His son has the wrong idea about God; somebody has told him lies and he's believed them.

— . . .

—They have a marvelous time that morning. Nothing would please me more than your recalling it.

—What are the lies, Mr. Ramirez?

—We'll discover them, if we keep a close eye on what's going to happen.

—What's going to happen?

—Larry, where do they go?

—They go out to look at their kingdom. To see how the Jews and everybody else are doing; to catalog sins—Sodom and Gomorrah—to give blessings, the Ten Commandments, create catastrophes, the flood . . . to rule.

— . . .

—That's what religion is about. An obsession with power. Power that no believer has, but worships in God. And God walks hand-in-hand with his son, showing him the whole fucked-up mess, and saying, "One day you'll have to clean this up. All by yourself."

— . . .

—"I'm going to send you down into that cesspool. You're going to clean it up." The son won't want to go, but his father will force him. The son will prefer to stay, under the protection of his father.

—The father will let him stay; the morning is not over. They still have time to enjoy themselves.

— . . .

—What else will they do? Will they play games? Will they read together?

—The father doesn't like to read, Mr. Ramirez.

—Do you think the son will be able to find out how to please God?

—The way to please God is to stay in line and do what he says, not to give him any trouble, not to disrupt things, but to stay in line.

—What does God enjoy doing?

—Dumb hobbies, puttering around, fixing things, nothing that requires too much smarts, or has much meaning, nothing of consequence.

—Maybe he would like to be taught something meaningful . . . consequential . . .

—What could that possibly be? . . .

—I don't know. He has limited abilities. He's trapped, too, in his narrow confines. By his own frustration at not being able to break out. And through transference he displays anger and annoyance when his son acts independently. God's authoritarian.

—The children are having a great time among themselves. What do you think they should teach him first?

—It's hard to say, hard to teach an old dog new tricks. It might make him cry. It might destroy him.

—But he wants to have a good time; he needs to. He may

die soon; he's old. Or worse, he's immortal; he's got to keep on living. . . . What do they do at night?

—Are you giving up on the morning, Mr. Ramirez?

—It's over. Night has come and time is running short. Something must be done to turn this difficult, somber day into a happy one.

—You're always concerned with happiness. There isn't that much happiness to be had.

—What is his face like?

—God's face?

—Yes.

—It's hard, with lines. With large features, but it's soft, too. It's strong and it's soft. It's hard and it's gentle. I liked both sides of him; he was my friend. I don't know what more I wanted from him. But there was something, nothing that he didn't give. He didn't give that much, but his kindness meant a lot, meant so much; I don't know what I wanted from him.

—Did you picture God with a familiar face?

—He had blue eyes. Sometimes they were hard and cold. Big nose, big cheeks and chin. He was balding; he had big hairy hands.

—When weren't his eyes hard and cold?

—You couldn't predict. That's what caused the problem. He didn't know why he went through changes which seemed arbitrary, whimsical. We didn't understand him. We liked him very much, but he disappointed us.

—Is there any way to make him happy tonight, something, a game that would make you happy, too, before it's time to sleep?

— . . .

—Was there something you both enjoyed a lot?

— . . .

—Something you enjoyed doing together?

—Maybe if he took me out someplace, without my

mother, someplace new, where we could both have fun together. If he had shared more of himself, it would have been easier.

—I think there's not much time left; it's late, Larry. Soon it will be time to go to bed. Please, something must be done right away so the day . . .

—It's all right, we'll live, you don't have to be perfectly happy.

—Larry, my capacity for happiness has greatly diminished. Please tell me what I can do to please him.

—I've already told you. Stay in line. Don't cause trouble. That will make him happy.

—I never meant to cause any trouble.

—From what I've read of your diaries you caused your share. It was beautiful.

—You're trying to confuse me.

—No, I admire what you did. You stood up against a monstrous repressive machine.

—I don't want to cause trouble, all I want is to see his blue eyes change, Larry . . . they look at me . . .

—You want to see the twinkle in his eyes. . . . Look, why do you need a father? You rule your own life.

—I'm exhausted. . . . I'm falling asleep . . . and you may work on my books; you won't disturb me . . .

—Thanks very much . . . I sure appreciate it.

—I'm a nobody, why should you thank me like that? . . . I haven't done anything.

—Mr. Ramirez, let me be honest with you. It revolts me to see you weak and pathetic. It's ridiculous . . . you stood your ground against incredible odds; you were strong. What happened to that person? I'd like to know and talk to him . . . not his substitute. . . . You're not Mr. Ramirez. . . . Where is he, what happened to him? Who are you?

— . . .

—You fought the enemy; you didn't run away from the battle . . .

—I don't want to cause trouble . . . if I did, he'd look at me again with those cold, hard eyes . . .

—What are you doing here?
—Nothing, working on your books. You kept falling asleep.
—Oh . . . I'm sorry.
—You slept for more than an hour.
—I didn't realize it. Last night I slept very little.
—You also didn't want to admit that I was proving something to you. Never mind, I'll keep working at this.
—No, please don't . . .
—Why not?
—Talk to me instead.
—Only if we talk about the same subject, Mr. Ramirez.
—Speak up, please.
—O.K., you worked very hard at your profession, didn't you? I guess you were a lawyer to begin with, specializing in labor law. You must have been very diligent, painstaking, patient, the way you keep notes here, the way you apply yourself to your encyclopedia. You had an academic background like me. And you acquired your work habits with difficulty. But there came a point when you loved to work, when it was no longer painful, when dealing with books and abstractions and subjects divorced from daily life was pleasurable, comfortable. Isn't that so?

—I guess you're right. But what's wrong with that?
—Nothing, but good things can be dangerous, seductive. Because of your accomplishments, and because you did socially productive work, your mind could legitimately unburden itself of difficult tasks. You sacrificed your family for your work, you avoided dealing with your wife and children and coping with their concrete daily needs, their demands on you. And that won't let you live in peace now.

—You're inventing all this. You have no way of knowing.
—It's what you wrote; it's in your prison notebooks.

—You're making it all up. It's your father who didn't pay attention to you. Or better . . . I only know that you accuse him of it. I'd like to hear what he has to say.

—You don't have flaws, yet you're guilty. How is that?

—I'm afraid, which is different. I have little strength left to defend myself.

—You're guilty, that's why you're afraid.

—That may be true of you. Yes, Larry. What are you guilty of?

— . . .

—If you tell me, maybe I'll be able to remember my own flaws. I won't be ashamed to admit them. But I need your help.

—I already told you. I'm guilty of lusting after my mother, of wanting to take her away from my father, of not caring what became of him, of throwing him out in my mind, letting him wander and starve, killing him—it didn't matter—anything to get him out of the way. Someone I loved, but wanted to destroy to satisfy my own needs. And, yes, take, steal his property, seize what was rightfully mine.

—You say that at the slightest opportunity; you're so quick to say that. You have ready-made phrases. Is that what the shrinks tell you to get rid of you? Or do you think it's amusing? Isn't it terribly unpleasant, and inaccurate besides?

—It's what they tell me my problem is. I tend to believe them.

—Is that the most disturbing thing you can think of? Or is there something worse?

—When I was a kid my mother told me this story that when I was a baby, I was very skinny and ugly; I looked like a monkey; I had long hair growing on the nape of my neck; I was so ugly that both she and my father were repelled, but they kept me anyway. I was coming back from school one day when two kids passed me; they laughed and said I looked like a monkey. I was really hurt and said no I didn't.

My mother had told me her story several months before and this seemed to confirm it.

—Is that the most harrowing thing you can think of?

—I'm sure there are others more terrifying. Buried.

— . . .

—There is this film called *The Incredible Shrinking Man*. A man is on a yacht, a small yacht, a pleasure cruiser. And he sails through fog, or mist, rising from the water out of nowhere. It's a beautiful movie. It's maybe a sunny Sunday. He's with a buddy; he's happy. Out of nowhere comes this cloud; and they pass through it and they say "Strange, what's that?" He's married; he has a very attractive wife; he's handsome himself. A very handsome couple, perfectly matched, in terms of intelligence, looks and size. Perfectly matched, beautiful couple, and they're happy together. He begins to discover his clothes are a little too big; his shirt collar is loose, his suit too baggy. Maybe he has lost some weight. But there's further shrinkage, and he notices his cuffs are a little long. And he becomes shorter than his wife. At this point he gets very anxious. His wife is supportive, and constantly reassures him of her love. He becomes upset, extremely irritable; starts snapping at his wife. Seeks medical advice. At one point he has to fend off a pussycat, who is now gigantic, prehistoric, compared to him. It's like being robbed of his masculinity, because his wife is always there. And the process continues until he's tiny. It's a very gripping movie; it's like the materialization of a depressive psychological state that we all recognize.

—I don't lust after my mother. I want to remember her face. I want to touch her. Does that mean I lust after her?

—I don't know.

—Do you think my son wanted to kill me, too?

—Yes. My father was not a man like you, he was a laborer. He was illiterate, inarticulate, simple, even stupid, and the thought of displacing him produced tremendous guilt in me.

Imagine the guilt your son must have felt for wanting to displace a man like you. A man whose qualities he perhaps thought he could never match.

—You know . . . those so-called notes you've been reading . . . I don't believe a word of them . . . those words belong to a novel, a very old one, too. You're reading and seeing in them what you like . . . and this is not an accusation . . . I'm really very grateful for your efforts.

— . . .

—You even lie so as not to make me feel inferior. I know about the superiority of your parents. I know the mistakes mine made, and it would delight me to hear about the mistakes your parents didn't make.

—It seems they made every mistake in the book. I remember only a few good times.

—You're too considerate with me. You can't display your riches, describe your fond memories. But I have a solution. Tell me about your parents as if they were mine. Tell me about my wonderful mother and father.

— . . .

— . . .

—O.K., Mr. Ramirez.

—First my mother.

—One day your mother took you to the zoo. She was very happy that day. She got dressed up, fixed her hair, and wore makeup. You thought she looked very pretty. She was milling about and vivacious, wouldn't stop chattering. You and she conversed, discussed this and that. That's what you liked most, when she actually talked to you, the way I see some mothers doing now with their kids . . . on the bus or subway. You were going to the zoo, and you took the subway to the Bronx. It was a very long ride, but she was not impatient or grumpy, because you were yakking all the way.

—About what?

—I remember your asking her for Kleenex and chewing

gum, and her opening her pocketbook and giving them to you. "Mom, can I have some gum?" . . . She was so happy and you didn't know why; you were overjoyed that she could be happy with just you, that you were good company to her.

—I don't remember that happy day; please tell me more.

—Later both of you walked the streets of Manhattan. You were holding hands, and she was still laughing and talking away.

—Why?

—You were like partners.

—Did she eat sweets?

—You remember pleasing her on only one other occasion. It was a rainy day. A small apartment. You had to stay in together. She complained to you about the landlord, not enough heat, too much rent, that kind of thing. But it didn't matter that she was complaining, just that she was confiding in you, sharing things with you. For a while you played with some toys on the floor. Then you went into the kitchen for a snack and both of you talked to each other some more. It was very warm and cozy that day, with the rain and just the two of you inside.

—I thought we lived in a house.

—Before that you lived in a small apartment. That same night your father came home and brought you a present. I think it was a record, maybe my first. I was very excited about it.

—*My* first record, and *I* was very excited about it.

—You must have hugged him and kissed him. He was happy, too. They both were. It must have given them pleasure to see you so excited about something they had given you. And evidently things were good between them; you picked that up, too. What an old memory; those times were so rare.

—What was the record?

—You always want to know the dumbest details.

—Then tell me what was the best present my father ever gave me. I can't remember.

— . . .

—Larry, let's see . . . I'm not necessarily talking about a real present; it could have been some advice he gave me. You can remember that, at least.

—Believe me, advice is not important. Words are not important. Intelligence is not important.

—What is?

—How a child feels he's regarded by his parents, and how he feels they regard themselves. Whether they're pleased with him. Whether he makes them proud. All their feelings about their son and themselves . . . are picked up by the child as reflections of himself. . . . And he can make mistakes and believe that his own image is what he sees when he looks down into that sewer.

—Does the child see himself when he looks into that putrid mess?

—It's out of those lights and shadows that he has to create his soul. Not with the help of any fucking advice.

—I want to touch my parents. Would that mean that I love them?

—Yes.

—Where should I touch them, for them to be pleased with me?

—Anywhere.

—You're withholding information from me; I know there are mistakes not to be made.

—I have never told so much to anyone.

—Please don't let me make any mistakes.

—You're bound to.

—I want to touch my mother.

—She's dead. She's been dead for a long time.

— . . .

—But she's in you, somewhere, Mr. Ramirez.

—I don't understand what you are saying; all I want to know is where to touch her.

—You make everything too simple.

—I want to kiss her where her thoughts are, on her forehead . . . and where her heart is . . . and my father's hand . . . I want to kiss it . . . because his hand is tired . . . from lifting the dies . . . and removing the paper, and stacking it . . .

— . . .

—Would it please my mother if I kiss her where her kind thoughts are? . . . Where her tender feelings are . . . there in her heart?

—I don't understand you.

—My father brought me a record as a present, you just told me. . . . So there are kind thoughts behind his forehead, too . . . and I should kiss my father's heart . . . for having loved her . . . and I should kiss my father's sex . . . for having given me my life. . . . My father gave me my life. . . . He made me in his image. . . . But why?

—He didn't think of you. Not at all.

—And I should kiss her hands . . . her hands are tired, too. . . . She's been working all day . . . in the house. . . . And I should kiss her belly, where she carried me . . . and her sex . . . that let me come out. . . . Or would that mean I lust after her, according to your system of instant analysis? . . . After hearing your lies about my lusting for her I now feel guilty without reason. You're deliberately undermining me.

—Behave yourself, or the Mafia will come and interrogate you.

—Please, don't ever repeat that word again. It frightens me to no end.

—Why?

—There's always some reference to it in the papers. It occurred to me that the Mafia might come to interrogate me for some reason, and they would not believe that I don't remember anything. They have no pity. It seems they're ruthless, like the Final Judgment. It is possible they'll suspect me of some crime. But what crime?

— . . .

—And what would they suspect you of? If you tell me, then I'll remember—as always—what I've been accused of . . .

—The crime is not specific. It's just a feeling, all-pervasive. You know you're guilty, but you don't know why. You feel the same way, too, Mr. Ramirez. That's why you're always imagining that someone will rob you. Or steal a look at your notes. Or your books. The purpose has vanished, the act committed, but guilt spreads over your life like an oil slick.

—The night is dark. So is this hospital room. My room at the home is not as dark; it has a larger window. Larry sneaks through that window at night to scare me. The first hours of the morning are the darkest. It is forbidden to look at the clock during the night. If it is four in the morning, there are about four more hours until daylight; if it is two, the night before is closer than the coming day. "Loneliness is a bad counselor," the Virgo nurse once said. Were her intentions good or bad? One cannot ask Larry because he doesn't know either. Security at the main entrance is strict, so one should not fear the entrance of undesirable persons into the hospital. It would be impossible to come through a window on the fifteenth floor. If it is two in the morning one is closer to the night before than to the coming day.

—You and your complaints.

—Hey? . . . What are you doing there?

—I was sleeping peacefully on the carpet when you woke me up with your litany.

—One of these nights you're really going to frighten me to death.

—Don't be such a baby.

—How did you come in?

—Who cares? Why waste time with meaningless details? We have much more urgent matters to consider.

—No doubt.

—Since I'm here in person, do you remember this little animal? We saw it together one day.

—Turn on the lamp, the one with less glare.

—All right . . . do you recognize it or not?

—Yes . . . certainly . . .

—You shouldn't lie to me, Mr. Ramirez.

—There's no reason for me to lie . . . I remember it very

well, it's the dog that woman was walking in Washington Square, the woman who smiled and was carrying a baby.

—You get an A.

—It impressed me; it was so white and furry.

—Don't make such expansive gestures; remember you're in an oxygen tent.

—Oh yes . . . you're right; I hadn't realized it.

—It must have been during the night . . . your gasping for breath must have alerted the doctors, and they put you back in the tent.

—The doctor and nurses. Curious they didn't trip over you and the dog.

—Why do you tremble so?

—I'm so cold; my feet are frozen.

—Do you need another blanket?

—They refused to give me one, and there's none in the closet. What's more, I can't call the night nurse because he would discover your presence.

—The carpet was warm, I slept quite comfortably, Mr. Ramirez.

—This dog has kind eyes.

—Yes, I see you made a good impression on it. That's why it approaches you. Doesn't it smell very clean, like warm soft wool?

—Yes.

—It's a nice animal. That's why it approaches you so timidly. Its paws are impeccably clean, and out of its mouth issues warm air, a little odorless steam, like a good little radiator.

—It has gently put one paw on my bed, as if it were asking for permission.

—If you caress the back of its neck, it'll know that it's welcome and will raise its other paw, too.

—You can feel warm skin under the hair on its neck.

—The animal is protected by its skin; its four paws are

clean and when it's on the bedspread it doesn't soil it. The animal is rather light, but very warm; it cuddles up to your feet and gives off heat. Soon you won't be cold anymore.

—It's like a fur blanket, very white. And extremely pleasant.

—The animal might appreciate your petting him, as a sign of approval.

—But, Larry . . . since I first started stroking its neck I haven't stopped petting this remarkably tame animal.

—I'm just worried about the owner, she must think that her dog is lost.

—And the baby. The baby must also miss this nice animal. But look, Larry, it's female . . . look at its teats, still rosy from having suckled its puppies.

—That cold morning the owner was taking this animal for a walk, along with the baby. The owner was smiling.

—The dog looks at me with her mouth open, with pointed ears and bright eyes. She shows me her teeth, like people do when they smile.

—If you dare, take one hand out of the tent and pet the nice animal, it's what she expects.

—Didn't I pet her already?

—Can't you hear this poor dog whining? She's already old, and tired, even more tired than you, Mr. Ramirez.

—More tired than me? That's impossible.

—This dog is much older than you, I'm sure. I can tell the age of animals by their teeth.

—I don't dare . . . stick my hand out.

—The dog is whining piteously, the poor thing.

—Won't I upset her, with my cold hand?

—I dare say not, Mr. Ramirez.

—What soft fur! I think I've already caressed this animal . . . many years ago. . . . Yes! Now I remember! Somebody was leading me by the hand to the park. That ancient tree was there. And she led me by the hand, that woman, the one who smiled and assured me that she would never leave me. And it was snowing, but I had insisted time and again that she take me to the park. And just when she was swearing that she'd never leave me, she dropped dead.

—It's not true. You're always afraid and imagining things.

—I'm not cold in the snow; I'm not complaining. Why do you scold me?

—You're both cold and hungry.

—Not at all, because her soft rosy teats are warm and the milk quells my hunger.

—She has no more milk to give you; her final days are nearing.

—Larry . . . I hear a slight noise, as if somebody were scratching at the door.

—You're right; let's see who it is . . .

—How peculiar, another dog of the same breed. It's wounded . . .

—No, it's limping, but from old age. And this one is male. And as old as the female.

—But his paws are dirty, I won't let him jump on the bed.

—Their breed is tame; you shouldn't be afraid. This animal is dying; I've never seen a more tired creature in my life.

—Maybe this oxygen . . . will revive him . . .

—No, you're much younger, Mr. Ramirez. If one of you must die let it be the older one.

—Seeing this dog is heartbreaking, Larry. I feel so much like caressing him. Bring him closer to me.

—Even if he soils the sheets?

—It doesn't matter . . .

—They're an old couple, evidently.

—Larry, I know I love this dog because I want so much to caress him.

—Do you?

—It's impossible to explain. But the dog understands me

and that's enough for me. The female is sleeping; she knows that this is the moment when I have to caress the one that just came in.

—Can you lock this door from the inside?

—No, Larry, it has no bolt . . .

—Then we're finished . . . listen to those steps . . .

—Why? You have never before been so pale . . . who's coming?

—You were right . . . and I wouldn't listen to you . . . forgive my stupidity . . . now it's too late . . .

—Larry, I can hear footsteps, too. . . . No! They're ferocious men, crime written all over their faces . . .

—They're not a gang of kids . . .

—They're murderous thugs; the interrogation will be only a farce.

—Maybe what you said about the Mafia was true.

—Murderers, Larry, that's the only thing that counts. It doesn't matter which gang they belong to.

—They're staring at you. You're the one they want, they pushed me into a corner. . . . But what a masterful attack by that dog that seemed to be on the verge of dying!

—He's already knocked the most menacing one over . . . he's biting him; he's sunk his sharp teeth into his filthy jugular vein!

—And the female . . . I'd say she's even more ferocious; she's got the other petrified . . . the thugs are in a quandary . . . they won't escape . . . and the male's about to pounce on them . . . the female keeps them cornered so the male can take aim. Before they realize it, they're bleeding to death, one, then the other . . .

—Yes, it's over for them . . . the two champion dogs drag the limp bodies out of the room . . . everything is again as it should be . . .

—But this is their last achievement, Larry, listen to them

gasping for breath, those poor old dogs. They defended me as if I were one of their offspring.

—Mr. Ramirez . . . maybe some oxygen would revive them . . .

—The doctor told me not to leave the oxygen tent even for a minute . . .

—Mr. Ramirez . . . they're dying . . . all that's left is the death rattle . . .

—Larry . . . bring the female over here . . . her first . . . let's try to save her . . . I can't watch her die like that . . . I'd rather risk my own life . . .

—Yes, I'll bring her to you . . .

—And as soon as she's revived bring me the male . . .

—No . . . no . . . what's happening?

—How'd the window get open?

—She has leapt into empty space . . . from the top floor . . .

—And the male has followed suit! . . . Larry, it's not my fault . . . don't look at me that way!

—I know you wanted to save them . . .

—They sacrificed themselves so that I would live . . .

—Those poor animals knew how to take care of their own.

—Oh . . . it's you . . . I thought that by now you had decided not to come . . .

—Yeah . . . listen . . . I know I'm a little late . . . I had lunch with my friend at Columbia . . .

—You accepted the job . . .

—No . . . not that. . . . He's very excited about your books and my working on them.

—Books?

—Yeah, your prison notebooks. He also called Montreal.

—I've never seen you like this before. You seem happy.

—Well, look, it might be good for me. I hope you don't mind my having the books. It might be the break I need . . .

—What's all the commotion . . . you're acting like a monkey . . . but you're not going to make me laugh; were I to laugh it would be bad . . . for my ribs . . . please . . . stop it.

—Look, you'll get recognition, too . . . with your human rights involvement. They're very interested.

—Oh, please, stop it . . . don't jump . . .

—Jesus, I'd like to see you laugh . . .

—No . . . it would hurt . . . I won't look at you . . . for a moment. It would hurt, you know, my ribs must be all cracked . . .

—If this thing gets off the ground there will be articles about you in magazines, books even.

—It sounds boring to me, but if it makes you happy go ahead, do what you want.

—Wait, let me get a drink of water . . .

—Oh . . . not that jumping around again. . . . Why are you behaving this way? It's ridiculous . . .

—My throat's dry. I called my friend at Columbia about your books. And those cryptic notes.

—Who?

—Remember I had a job interview last week? Well, that didn't work out. But I kept the number, and this morning I thought he'd be the right person to call about your books and notes . . .

—So . . .

—He got very excited, asked me to meet him for lunch. He was waiting for me at the History Department office; he had called Montreal . . .

—What's that? What's in Montreal?

—The Institute for Latin American Studies at the university there. There's a project going on concerning political repression in Latin America. . . . My friend at Columbia didn't want to let the cat out the bag, but, in Montreal, they're studying political repression from the time of Spanish colonialism to today . . . and they need contemporary material; it's perfect.

—I don't understand; your friend wanted the material but called Montreal. . . . It doesn't make sense.

—Yeah . . . he himself doesn't have the kind of money to fund such a project. He wanted to help me so he called a friend in Montreal.

—He sounds like a very fair person.

—Yeah, he is. We had a huge lunch, and got carried away. Had a little too much to drink; that's why I'm late.

—He sounds like a very generous man.

—Well, he'll get something out of it, too. The man in Montreal offered something in exchange. Apparently, there are charters dating back to the French period that have never left the university. He offered to lend them to Columbia. It's a big coup for my friend.

—But why are you so ecstatic?

—I'm developing a lot of contacts. And there's the chance I might be published. Then there's the money, and maybe permanent work.

—All that?

—Yeah, all that.

—How wonderful! This is something we really didn't expect.

—Yeah, finally a break.

—Go ahead; take the books; you have the key.

—Later. I'm supposed to take care of you now.

—What?

—From two to four you pay me to take care of you. I can't wheel you around, so let's talk.

—Of course. It's Monday.

—How about you? Are you feeling any better?

—I don't know.

—You're seeing better today, aren't you?

—Yes . . . I hadn't realized it. . . . I'm feeling better, yes . . . thank you.

—That's good. And less paranoid . . . I'm only kidding. I thought of you today at lunch. For dessert the professor had crepes with whipped cream. I know how much you love sweets, and I'm sure you would have wanted a taste. Maybe when you get better you can enjoy desserts again.

—Since so much fuss is made about Christmas, I'd like something sweet then.

—Maybe a little piece of something sweet won't kill you. By the way . . . I saw a lunch tray by your door, outside, in the corridor, almost untouched.

—Yes, it was mine; I wasn't hungry at all.

—You should eat, shouldn't you?

—Yes, but I didn't feel like it. Larry . . . isn't Christmas tomorrow?

—I'd like to use your books all day tomorrow; will you be busy? If not we could spend some time bullshitting.

—Busy, me?

—Maybe somebody from the committee is coming . . .

—You're being polite. . . . You know I'll be alone all day.

—Well, then we can gab during my breaks. Do you play chess?

—I don't like to be silent. No. Not while you're here.

—I should have guessed. Were you always so chatty?

—The other day you started to tell me about the girl with the name of the cheese, and then we dropped her entirely.

—I used to walk past her house five times a day on week-ends . . . hoping she would be sitting on the stoop, so I could wave and go over and talk to her. One Saturday afternoon she was actually there. I almost fainted . . . from the excitement. My body actually started to shake, and I could feel my legs growing weaker by the second. Do you want to hear more?

—You know I do.

—You're a voyeur, Mr. Ramirez. A dirty old man. But I'll go on. She was sitting on the stoop, and I went over and started talking to her about school. She was sitting and I was standing. She was wearing a low-cut halter, and from where I was standing I could almost see her breasts. You can imagine my excitement.

—No, I can't. That's why I want to hear more.

—It's something special to see the body of someone you love . . . for the first time. I can hardly describe it. Her breasts were milky white, with freckles; and her nipples were pink. Do you know what young girls' breasts are like before they've been fondled?

—Yes, they're milky white, with freckles, and the nipples are pink.

—They change shape after they've been fondled. Did you know that? A man's body, too. You can tell when a person walking down the street has not yet had sexual relations.

—Really?

—I think so.

—What do you mean?

—I don't know. . . . The excitement of that situation was

too much for me. I was an awkward adolescent. Very attracted to this girl, wanting to slip my hand down her blouse, right there on the spot. I had to hold that feeling in check while we talked about problems at school, and she smiled. Imagine how shitty you feel when someone is speaking to you about something mundane, and smiling, and all you can think about is shoving your hand down her blouse. It makes you feel subhuman. Everyone else goes about their business; it's shameful. And you try to hide that part of yourself.

—Tell me the good things, by now I can well imagine the bad ones.

—What do you want to know?

—The joys she gave you.

—I already told you.

— . . .

—I finally got up enough nerve to ask her for a date. She accepted. We went to a movie. The movie was mediocre; neither of us cared for it. I was very uptight that night, rigid, self-conscious. It was torture. I was glad when it was over.

— . . .

—There's a terrible excitement . . . the first time that one's sexuality . . . repressed, because of the attraction to one's own mother, tries to free itself . . . of those connotations, and attach itself to a new object . . .

—What happened the next time you saw the Dorman girl?

— . . . There are few actual encounters with girls at that age. And sex is not talked about with girls, but with other boys. It's not thought of as gentle or as giving pleasure to girls. Boys talk about it among themselves as a nasty, lecherous impulse they share, as opposed to girls, and as opposed to school authorities, who forbid it, never give it recognition, and are always talking about drier subjects. There's solidarity among boys because they share these impulses and don't imagine that girls have the same feelings. If a girl actually agreed to do something . . . she immediately degraded herself in our eyes. And became less desirable as a sexual object.

—What happened the next time you saw the Dorman girl?

— . . .

— . . .

—We were very afraid of girls, and thought more about their breasts than any other part of their bodies.

—But one day, it was all resolved. Right now, I need to hear about it as desperately as when I longed for sweets while I had the fever.

— . . .

—One day all problems were solved, Larry.

— . . .

— . . .

—O.K., Mr. Ramirez. I met my wife-to-be at a party when I was seventeen years old. We were both in high school then. She was very tall and stately for a high-school girl. She had fine aquiline features, high cheekbones, a thin nose, a well-sculpted head. She had blond hair, and she wore it in a French twist, the formal style of the day. She was very simply dressed and had a good figure. But her clothes were modest, not sexy. Her propriety made her more alluring. The attraction was instantaneous. We were so used to Italian girls, with large coarse features, big haunches in tight-fitting skirts. Or Irish girls! With puke-white skin and freckles, frizzy hair, misshapen bodies, and a funny smell. It seemed that I had never seen someone so fine. I think that she was attracted to opposite qualities in me. Sleek, Latin, dark flashing eyes, etc.

—It's strange that you should mention your eyes; I think they are small and darting.

—Yeah, I know. Now they're a little dull. But when I was an adolescent, they flashed.

—What was her favorite topic of conversation? How were you able to guess it so quickly?

—We hit if off perfectly. We were fascinated by our differences. We would neck on the back porch late at night for hours. When I went home each night my balls hurt.

—You were talking about that first party.

—We danced together several times that night. I wanted to dance with only her, and kept a close watch on the other guys who asked her. Dancing every dance with her would have been too forward and obvious, and I would have made myself obnoxious. So you had to let a few dances go by, when you danced with other people. But had to ask her again periodically, so that you would become a presence in her evening. The last dance also, I had to dance with her. To consolidate what came before and get her phone number, so that I would be able to see her again. I knew she was pleased, too, and I went home that night, light as a bird. I don't remember what I dreamt.

—What was her favorite topic of conversation?

—I don't know, we talked about everything. I was so cocky and cocksure at that time. I read voraciously, and could bullshit about many things.

—You hadn't been able to bullshit with that other girl.

—That's right. Something liberated me this time. I don't know what it was.

—You can remember, if you try.

—It's not about remembering, Mr. Ramirez. I'd have to figure it out now, for the first time.

—You said she was different from the others, not only physically.

—There was something asexual about her. She was a virgin, innocent, naive. She was yet to be awakened as a sexual being. And perhaps that relaxed me. It enabled me to come on strong, sexually. To play the aggressor, knowing that she would most likely resist. It liberated the masculine in me. Does that satisfy you, you prying bastard?

—I'm not a prying bastard; you should use other words if you want to describe me accurately.

—I've tried, nothing seems to stop you.

—This is maybe the first pleasant subject that you have discussed with me; don't you feel like continuing?

—No, not really. It feels like work.

—What was her favorite topic of conversation?

—She didn't have one. We talked about so many things. It's beautiful to discover someone, their intelligence and sensibility, when you already have something invested in them.

—You quickly found out what her favorite things were. How did you do it?

—I did not. Please don't put words in my mouth.

—Of all the boys in New York she chose you. You must have found out what pleased her.

—She chose me because her experience was limited; even after ten years of marriage, that's how I thought of it. That I was lucky, that she became attached to me early, before she saw what the whole field had to offer. And I expected that someday she would find out and leave me, find out that I held on to her by ruse and guile. I never believed enough in myself to believe in her love for me, even after ten years. I'm sorry I can't supply the fairy tales you want to hear.

—Then what qualities did you admire in her?

—Her gullibility . . . and her beauty.

—Once you mentioned not feeling complete without a woman. I listened, but didn't really grasp the meaning. If I did, maybe I'd understand many more things. Can you think of a moment when you felt complete in those days?

—Not off the top of my head. Besides, I don't remember saying that.

—Maybe you used different words.

—I said I had a nagging sense of incompleteness, a strong yearning, a feeling that something was missing, and I tried to satisfy it with a woman.

—I believe I understand incompleteness. I'd like to hear about completeness now.

— . . .

—I want to learn what you feel when you say, "I'm complete."

—I don't remember saying that . . . we used to spend long Sunday afternoons together. After a week of school, days, classes, nights, homework, Saturday's chores, Sunday at last. I'd meet her around noon or one o'clock, after she came back from church, and we'd make a picnic, go to the park. From midafternoon till evening, we'd watch it grow dark. The colors around us would change, the first stars would appear. . . . It was a big, beautiful park, more like a forest than a park, and when you were inside you couldn't see the dreary apartment buildings surrounding it. All you could see were hills and pine trees. We'd bring a blanket, some food, books to read. We would talk and kiss, take walks, read favorite passages aloud to each other . . .

—From which books?

—No . . . no, I don't remember. It was so long ago. It doesn't seem that it could ever happen again. It seems like the only time I was ever happy.

—I'm curious. Are you sure you don't know what her favorite topics of conversation were?

—No, I don't remember that she had any.

—You must hurry up now, she must be waiting. The afternoon is short. Is she waiting for you in the park?

—She used to wait for me at home. She was never ready. Her mother would always answer the door. And I would have to wait a half-hour, while she put on makeup, before coming downstairs. It was always exciting when I saw how she looked. And what she was wearing.

—What is she wearing today?

—This happened twenty years ago.

— . . .

— . . . A blue silk blouse. And you get a whiff of perfume

as you enter the room. At the time I used to like that; but
now when a woman wearing perfume steps into an elevator
with me I gag. Only women do that, spend time making
themselves up.

—What is in the picnic basket?

—Sandwiches and cake.

—What color is the forest?

—Green and blue.

—Is there anyone around?

—A few people, but we find an isolated spot. You can
only see forest; you can't see the city surrounding it; you're
free on Sundays. Most people were off from work; we were
off from school, which amounted to the same thing. We
weren't reminded of our lives in that park. We were free to
imagine anything.

—Like what?

—All the lives we could lead, all the things we could do.
Things that made our spirits soar.

—Just one of them . . .

—I don't remember.

—Being rich?

—I don't remember.

—Being somewhere else?

—Yes.

—Where?

—I don't remember.

—Really?

—Well, maybe Algeria. The desert. I remember reading
Camus; existentialism was big in those days. I read *The
Stranger*. The hot sand on the beach, the lazy waves and the
foam, the bronze bodies, the coolness of the evening. Him
looking down from his apartment at night, seeing the young
people, joking and laughing in the street, heading for bars
and movies. . . . I thought of how nice it would be to be in
Algeria. With the openness, and blazing sun, and the

bronzed young people that I would meet. . . . Later I found out he was talking about a colony. The bronzed young people were Europeans; they were hated, and soon to be ejected. But nobody was political in the fifties.

—Does she like Algeria, too?

—I don't know if I ever mentioned it to her.

—What are you doing with her in Algeria?

—We're walking on a deserted beach. It's sultry; the sun's scorching hot. It's uncomfortable. But we like it. We're getting darker, bronze. I push her down on a dune, and begin to take off her bathing suit. Should I stop here, Mr. Ramirez?

—It's getting dark in the forest; you may not find your way out later on.

—It's springtime, and it's a little chilly. But the necking is generating a lot of heat. I lie on top of her, and grind away. We used to call it a dry hump. It was very dry, until you came in your pants. Then the sand got all over us, clinging to perspiration, and we went into the sea, to wash off.

—You're trying to confuse me. You're in the forest, and you haven't undressed.

—Our honeymoon was in Cape Cod. We would go to a deserted beach, take off all our clothes. I could see the white V made by her bathing suit, and her shiny pubic hair, that looked so vital, that glistened and twinkled when she came out of the water. We made love on a dune, the sun was baking us . . . and the sand was scratchy, chafing our skin and making it red. The white juice would trickle down my tanned stomach, slow up when it got to the delta, then run quickly down my side.

— . . .

—The blue sky, and the hot sun . . . seemed so approving. I was young, and we would wait awhile and do it again and again . . . until I couldn't. Dinner in the evening was beautiful . . . and the wine.

—What was in the sandwiches in the picnic basket? I'm getting hungry.

—Nothing. A hole.

—You don't remember what was in the sandwiches. You shouldn't be ashamed to admit it. What's more, you shouldn't lie . . . because there is something in it.

—There is nothing. That's what makes it so mysterious.

—I shouldn't be so demanding with you. You've been kind enough to tell me so many things. By now you must be anxious to go and read the books that are in the locker. Go ahead, take them out.

— . . .

—Don't tell me you've lost the key.

—No, I haven't.

—I'll keep myself busy by eating something . . . I'm awfully hungry.

—Should I go and get you something, something sweet?

—No, I'll call the nurse. I want something that will agree with me.

—That's right, Mr. Ramirez.

—And just in case I fall asleep . . . even if you had a good lunch today with your Columbia friend . . . let me look for my wallet one second . . .

—No, please don't bother . . .

—Listen, Larry, go and have dinner at our restaurant. Otherwise you won't be able to tell me what is on the menu tonight, which happens to be Christmas Eve.

—Thank you, then.

—People also celebrate Christmas Eve, I believe.

—Yes, they do.

—I've been a fool, then, take twice as much and invite her, too.

—I'm going to dine alone tonight, as I do every night.

—Mr. Ramirez, wake up.

—What? . . . What's the matter?

—That's enough . . . I can't stand that tone. I won't tolerate it.

—I was resting . . . why did you wake me up so rudely?

—I had something to tell you, Mr. Ramirez, something of great urgency.

—So what are you waiting for?

—O—O.K. . . .

—Your voice is trembling, Larry.

—The northern night is so cold. You think I'm by your side because you can hear me speaking.

—But I don't see you, the darkness is total.

—Mr. Ramirez, for some strange reason you hear my words and can almost feel my breath, as if I were beside you. In reality I'm very far away, lost once again. I was on a train, going to Montreal, when I recognized some hostile faces.

—Don't make fun of me, Larry, you're here beside me.

—Turn the light on, and you'll see that I'm not.

—No, the light would hurt my eyes. Proceed with your prank.

—I jumped off the train and found myself in that same place you saw in the magazine. There was a lake between snow-capped mountains and Arctic vegetation, do you remember it?

—Yes. It was a color photo, an ad for a brand of cigarettes. I had been thinking about your phone call to Montreal and when I saw that Canadian landscape I made the association.

—Now you listen to me. I have no time to waste. I'm in great danger. The total darkness that envelops me does not permit me to take a step. I'm afraid of walking off a cliff.

—I know you're not faking it, your fear is real. What I don't understand is how your voice can reach me.

—I remembered how prisoners on death row are granted a last request before being executed, even if it's only a special dinner. And before falling into a chasm of icy air I requested . . . that you hear me.

—I remember the place perfectly, Larry, be careful, there are jagged rocks, etched against the clear blue sky. The blue of the lake is somewhat darker, but with shimmering reflections of sunlight that can blind you.

—Reflections of a cold Arctic sun. It will never rise for me again.

—No, it requires a little patience. I know that problem better than anybody. I often wake up in the middle of the night thinking that dawn will never come.

—I'm afraid of tripping and falling.

—The place is very clear in my mind; I've seen that ad many times. Follow my instructions.

—I'm listening.

—If you're standing up, slowly kneel down.

—O.K.

—Feel the ground with your hands.

—Yes. I'm touching a rock, it's smooth.

—Larry, you're at the entrance of a grotto. Listen closely and in the distance you'll hear the murmur of a spring.

—Yes, the farther I go the clearer I can hear the gurgling of the waters.

—You're entering into the grotto. It's less cold there.

—Yes, the air is becoming mild.

—We were lucky; you could have come into the landscape where the pines grow more densely, and where the snow makes passage impossible.

—Mr. Ramirez, the water in the spring is a little more than warm and a little less than boiling.

—Remove the chill from your bones, immerse yourself in it.

—Yes, my clothes, wet from the snow, are drying in the

warm air. I'm still shivering; I'm taking my shoes off; I'm unbuttoning this layer of clothes; my numb fingers hardly respond; my body feels like an old man's.

—You feel like I do; your joints are rusty; your muscles shriveled; your skin is thick as hide. But once you are in the spring the weariness of old age will vanish.

—Yes, my joints respond to any whim, my muscles flex with pleasure.

—Relax, Larry, float without fear; they are good waters.

—Is someone coming? Is a traveler approaching with a lantern? I think I see light right where I came in.

—It's the light of day. The entrance to the grotto lets it in.

—You were right; we left the night behind. Now I see that I must follow every one of your instructions.

—I'll try not to disappoint you. I was just lucky to see the landscape; it remained fixed in my mind.

—I have recovered the use of my body. I can head for the exit, and recuperate by eating something. But where can I find food?

—There are tree trunks floating in the lake; tie them up with strips of bark, venture into the water with a net made out of foliage stems and fish for the most delicious of trout.

—Mr. Ramirez, I want to know more about the landscape.

—The rocks are reddish brown, the peaks immaculate white.

—The trout are silvery, very tasty. When night falls I'll go back into the grotto, my hunger satisfied.

—Are you weary?

—Yes, but it's a tiredness that gives me . . . how can I put it? . . . a certain pleasure. I know that by taking a dip in the spring I'll become strong again.

—It's not clear whether you fell asleep last night while floating in those waters.

—It makes no difference, Mr. Ramirez. What counts is the repose.

—I'm very interested in the subject of falling asleep.

—Since I arrived in this landscape of lakes I fall asleep every night with no problem.

—Tell me more.

—Yes, Mr. Ramirez, looking for food makes the day go by quickly. Oh, I didn't tell you, I'm building a picturesque cabin way up there, with an unsurpassable view.

—Isn't the grotto good enough for you anymore?

—No, because during the day I like to take breaks in the sunlight. The grotto awaits me at night.

—What else, Larry? There are no problems left?

—Thanks to you, Mr. Ramirez, who showed me the way.

—You're always so considerate. But I detect in your voice a note of nostalgia; you can't fool me.

—I have no complaints. That's all I can complain about, not having complaints.

—But there's no joy in your words.

—Mr. Ramirez, I know what's on your mind, that I need a woman.

—Apparently.

—But it isn't so. They always gave me problems. They're extremely desirable, but I must admit that I'm afraid of them. At my age I should have solved this problem, but no, I'm still frightened of them. Better keep them at a distance, the divine creatures.

—Don't you feel carnal lust urging you on?

—I appease it with my hand.

—Excuse me for the indiscretion.

—Do you remember the landscape well? Mr. Ramirez, don't you find its extraterrestrial serenity enough?

—If you say so . . .

— . . .

—Larry . . .

—...

—Larry, answer me, or is it that I can't hear you?

—Yes ... you ... you can ... hear me.

—You're crying.

—...

—Larry, don't be like that, you worry me.

—The landscape is perfect, Mr. Ramirez, it's a manifestation of divine power. Someone created this rich and majestic serenity.

—I'm pleased that you say so; it must help you in your loneliness.

—No, Mr. Ramirez. I'm not the landscape.

—You can explore it.

—Yes, but I don't share its serenity, nor its richness, nor its majesty, nor any of its other qualities. The day that something, a hurricane, a tempest, sweeps me out of here, the landscape will remain impassive. Without me it will be as complete as ever.

—Larry, your voice sounds more and more anguished. It frightens me.

—...

—Larry ... say something ...

—...

—Larry, you're not wrong ... you're right ... at least know that ... that you're not wrong ... I don't have enough either. ... There was a moment of stupidity, when I prayed for recovery, agreeing to be content with eating and sleeping ... Larry, you're absolutely right ... I also want to be the landscape ... I want to flourish quietly, like a plant, or rush like an avalanche if movement is what I crave.

—Mr. Ramirez ... listen to me, although I have no strength left in my voice ... what you crave is power.

—No! ... Don't be obtuse ... you imbecile!

—What?

—Yes, you imbecile ... power is detestable ... God may

have that horrible problem, and I don't envy him. . . . What I want is . . . to feel something that I thought existed . . . but I don't know what it is . . .

—Mr. Ramirez, these are perhaps my last words, I have no strength left whatsoever. I don't want to save myself either, to find my way back to the grotto . . . I'll remain here; the snow will eventually cover me, and this will finish once and for all.

—No . . . please . . . who will come and talk to me if you die? This is an act of total selfishness. You must also think of me.

— . . .

—Larry . . . answer me . . .

— . . .

—If I could get there, I'd drag you into the grotto. After a dip you'd forget everything. . . . The worst is that a body that doesn't want to live becomes so heavy . . . I drag it, but I advance only a few inches at a time. There are branches blocking the path, yes, he chose the farthest point in the landscape, at the opposite end of the grotto, and for me such a task will prove impossible . . . and the night is so dark, and I don't know any shortcuts, and I'm unable to devise a strategy . . .

— . . .

—I don't remember requesting to be taken to this landscape as my last wish. The last wish of a condemned man. But it was granted to me, and that means there is a possibility of rescue. It's possible that he will be saved, but as for myself I doubt it . . . in this cold, in this inclement wind, and dragging such a burden . . .

—Please . . . continue . . . go ahead . . .

—What did you say? . . . I can't hear you . . .

—I know the way well by now, Mr. Ramirez. . . . What you must do is keep going . . . in the same direction . . . always straight ahead . . .

—Very well . . .

— . . . because it isn't much farther.

—I can't see anything, Larry, darkness is total in this Arctic night. Only when the air becomes warmer will I know that I'm inside the grotto.

—Thank you . . . thank you . . .

—I can already hear the gurgling water . . . I hope I'm not dreaming . . .

—Exactly . . . me, too . . . and the cold is no longer the same . . .

—But I have no strength left . . . up till now . . . I've been able . . . I've been able . . .

—Yes . . . tell me . . .

—I've been able . . . to . . . to . . .

—Thank you. We're safe now.

—Not me, Larry . . . I'm very weary . . . I won't live to see another day.

—You say that because your eyes are closed.

—I don't want to open them ever again.

—You'll change your mind, Mr. Ramirez.

—No . . . there's no time left.

—You're wrong, again. Open your eyes, and you'll get a surprise.

—No . . .

—Open them and you'll see something.

—Is someone coming, Larry? Is a traveler approaching with a lantern? I think I see light right where I came in.

—It's the light of day. The entrance to the grotto lets it in.

—No, a bit of dawn filters in through the hospital window. It's good to know that the night is over.

— . . .

—What a soothing silence . . .

— . . .

—If nobody calls me or asks for me, I might go back to sleep. Silence and solitude sometimes help people rest and recuperate after a very big effort.

—So this is Christmas.

—Yes . . .

—I don't know why I had this idea . . . that you would bring me some sweets, since it's a holiday . . . but now I'm glad you haven't; they're bad for me.

—Would you like a piece of apple?

—No . . . they brought me one already, a whole one, didn't you see it? I just ate it. . . . Thank you.

—Don't get too excited about Christmas; you'll be disappointed.

—All the personnel in this hospital seemed excited; why's that?

—They have families; they're going to go out and get drunk, who knows.

—Larry . . . will they all be disappointed in the end?

—No . . . some of them won't remember what happened.

—You made your way through many pages this morning; shouldn't you take a little rest?

—I'm not tired.

—Fine, we can chat a bit then.

—It's not fair . . . I'm always the one talking about my life; why don't you talk about yours?

—You already know all the gossip from the home. Here at the hospital I still haven't made one single acquaintance in four days. What else is there for me to say?

—You've lived for more than four days . . . tell me how you coordinated those wildcat strikes . . . at six plants, bypassing union leadership.

—Was that in the book? I don't believe it.

—It sure was. In the words of another century, though.

—You must be careful, boy. Maybe I was not telling the truth . . .

—Maybe we could talk about it a little.

—I must admit something. You'll think I'm an easy mark for advertisements, but I'm intrigued by Christmas. I saw so many advertisements on the street, in the days when you were wheeling me around . . . but above all else, yesterday and today . . . the excitement of the people here . . . really impressed me. I'd give anything to see what goes on in one of their homes, right now, at lunchtime . . .

—You're blowing the whole thing out of proportion. It's a holiday; people get the day off from work; they get drunk; they spend money; that's all.

—But all those presents they are buying, what happens when the boxes are all opened?

—The kids love it. It's a very special occasion for them.

—And the adults? What do they feel when the kids open their presents?

—It gives them pleasure, too.

—Larry . . . but if the presents are not for the adults, what gives them pleasure?

—You ask so many boring questions.

—I can understand the pleasure of opening your own box. But what you're supposed to feel when somebody else opens his present, that remains a mystery to me.

—The idea that you're supposed to feel something is often responsible for disappointments and depression. People like yourself have high expectations for the holidays.

—I had no expectations, but people infected me. It seemed they had good reason to expect a lot.

—What reason?

—That's what I don't know. But you said one shouldn't expect anything, in order to avoid disappointment. And it wasn't clear whether you meant the moment when you're opening your own box, or what.

—I think people enjoy giving, giving pleasure to others. It makes them feel good. As good as they feel when they're on the receiving end.

—Where is one supposed to feel the pleasure of giving? In the chest? The throat? . . . The eyes?

— . . .

—Oh . . . I know: in the hands. I can't use my hands in the oxygen tent.

—What are you talking about? Are you delirious?

—No, I was recollecting something; but I don't know what it was.

— . . .

—Excuse me, then . . . I'm sure you would prefer to talk about other things. One in particular pleases you no matter what the occasion.

—Which?

—The high-school girl with the fine aquiline features.

—I had forgotten about her, until you forced me to remember. It's funny how one buries even pleasant memories.

—Especially those, when it comes to you.

— . . .

—Larry, what happens on Christmas, when a young man is forced to spend the day with his parents, but would like to be with his girl instead? Would the girl be welcome at the boy's house?

—What are you talking about?

—May I be frank?

—Please.

—I'd like to know how this important holiday is celebrated at your house, among your dear ones, and I want to hear more about that lovely girl. Your girl was once at your house on Christmas. And you finally had everything you wanted.

—This is sickening.

— . . .

—Hmmm . . . you know, there was the occasion when she had to meet my parents for the first time. Especially my mother, whose approval was somehow very important to me.

—Yes . . .

—I was more worried about my mother's approving of my girl friend than about her approving of my mother. It's weird; it wasn't as if I would have stopped seeing her, if my mother hadn't liked her. But still my mother's approval was important to me. My girl looked so good that day. She was so gracious, so polite, so innocent, that even my mother was charmed. My parents couldn't stop talking about her. The only thing my mother didn't understand was why she chose me. It was like bringing a prize home to my parents.

—I'm not worried about your mother's approval, but about your father's. What is he doing right now?

—He's looking at her. And smiling. He likes the way she looks. He's beaming, in fact. He's all flushed. He's trying to be conversant; I've never seen him so social. It's good for him, for another woman to be brought into the house.

—I feel the same way.

—Yes, they're very pleased. She's so clean-cut and whole-some. And good looking, too. After all those tawdry Italian girls. My mother is bubbling over, too.

—Your father, he'd also like to give her a nice present . . . but he didn't remember in time. Anyhow, it doesn't matter, she does not expect anything from your father, or does she? And I'm afraid now. . . . This could be so embarrassing for him . . . he may have forgotten.

— . . .

—He wouldn't know what to get her . . . and he doesn't dare ask her. Larry, would you ask her on his behalf?

—Let him ask her himself.

—What did you buy for her? Or is it too early to open the boxes?

—Look, there were no presents. It wasn't Christmas; it was better than Christmas. Everyone was happy.

—Your father had no reason to be embarrassed then . . .

—No, of course not. He was never livelier, he was usually

glum; but this day he was almost gabby. Competing with my mother to get a word in edgewise. He was running around fixing drinks, playing the gracious host. My mother's testiness and crabbiness somehow vanished. She was all smiles. My little brother and sister were running up and down the stairs, catching second and third glimpses. And whispering and giggling to themselves.

—Does your father like her as much as I do?

—Yes, he likes her very much. More than he could perhaps ever admit to himself. He lusts after her.

—What does he say to her?

—He questions her about school, about her ambitions. And he's pleased . . . that she's a nice girl.

—He was going to ask her something, but he got so nervous about not bringing her a present . . . that . . .

—That what?

—He doesn't know anymore what to tell her.

—Let him say what he's thinking.

—Don't tell anybody, don't tell them . . . but there's a reason why he forgot to buy her a present . . . he got so nervous thinking about something else, he forgot all about her . . . that is . . . he got frightened . . . Larry, he knows what to feel when he opens his own present . . . but she'll realize he doesn't know what to feel when she opens hers . . .

—I don't follow you.

—He doesn't know what it is like to give a woman a present. He doesn't know what he's supposed to feel when she opens it.

—Presents don't interest me. I don't give any and I don't receive any. Besides, if I'd have to, I'd rather give one than receive one.

—We'll return to that point some other time. You're not generous, Larry. Let's go back to the main point; maybe the presents are to be opened at the end of the party. . . . That gives him time. . . . Is it a long party?

—As we sit down at the table to eat, Mr. Ramirez, the phone rings.

—Why are you looking at me like that?

—Because I'm in a difficult position. The caller is one of the workers at the union hall. The union leaders have just signed the contract with the owner. The workers don't like it, and are ready to strike. He wants me to come down immediately and organize it.

—You're not a working man, Larry.

—No, I teach sociology in college, but I'm an organizer, too. I've helped the workers before.

—Is nobody else able to help them?

—There are others, but they know me. They know I listen to them, instead of the union leaders. And I'll go as far as they want to go.

—You're busy, there's a party in your honor. Give them the name of some other organizer.

—The others would be afraid to get involved in this strike, for fear of crossing the leadership and getting shot. Besides, I'm a master tactician in difficult situations.

—What are you going to do?

—I have to leave right away.

—But your family will be hurt if you leave; they'll be disappointed.

—Yes, I have to say something . . . but what can I say?

— . . .

—What could I tell them, Mr. Ramirez, without hurting them?

—Are you sure nobody can replace you at the union hall?

—No one.

—And is there a valid reason to call the strike?

—Yes. The workers want it and they can win. That's enough, isn't it? What do you think?

—Are the workers' demands fair?

—Inflation is so high they can hardly eat.

— . . .

—What should I tell my family and my girl friend? How can I leave and not offend them?

—I'd like so much to help you, Larry . . . but it's hard for me . . .

—You have to help me . . . I must go to the union hall . . . now! It's crucial, they need my help to win. If they lose there'll be reprisals.

—Maybe . . . you should talk to your girl friend separately . . . then to your mother . . . or to your father . . .

—But what do I tell them? How can I leave without offending them?

—You always say your girl friend is quite sensible; I would talk to her first.

—But she's going to be hurt. This is a very special day, the first time she's met these people; she needs me there for support. But I must go. What can I say to her?

—You should give her a reason for what you're doing. A reason that she can understand. Well, you see . . . for her, nobody could take your place. So all you should have to explain to her is the reason that for those workers you're irreplaceable, too.

—That's good. She's irreplaceable also, but even if she understands, and she will, of course, even if she sees that it's necessary, and agrees that I should do it, she'll still feel hurt that I left her there.

—Maybe not, not if she's made to understand why you're irreplaceable. Go ahead and tell her the secret, she won't betray you.

—It's happened before, you know. When I had to leave her in various situations. Will she want a life with someone like me? Do I have the right to ask her to stay with me?

—If she's the way you have described her to me, she'll feel

good supporting you in this case. But you must tell her the secret.

—What secret?

—The reason you are the only one who can do the job.

—The workers want to strike, close down the plant for a month, but they'll suffer too much from the loss of wages. They may lose the strike; the owners can hold out. I think there's a better way. I must convince them.

—You will convince her, too, if you explain your plan.

—The workers are in contact with a clandestine organization. They have the production plan for the whole plant. There are thirty departments. If each stops working at a specific time, two hours a day for one week, management's losses would be as great as if everyone stopped working for a month. The workers would lose very little in salary, and the owners would not be able to economize on wages or electricity. That's my master plan. I have to convince them that it can work.

—Not two hours a day, Larry, but just two hours twice a week would suffice. What matters most is how precise each department is. The job action must totally disrupt the production process. You see, a production plan follows a logical sequence; it's that sequence that must be botched. ... If the pieces produced in a certain section aren't removed in time, they will pile up and jam the assembly line. Another example: if the axles aren't worked on, the production process will come to a halt.

—I think that'll convince her.

—It did, Larry. I saw the way she was listening to you. She understood everything perfectly.

—What can I tell my father?

—Talk to your mother first.

—But what can I say to her? She's not much interested in union matters. She suspects that it's all Communists' plots.

—If there's no time to explain things to her . . . maybe you could tell her that it's too late for you to withdraw from the fight. If your people don't win, your enemies will come and destroy you. It's a matter of life and death. If the group doesn't fight, she'll lose her son.

—That's good.

—But assure her you'll be back tonight. There's no danger at this meeting. Nobody knows you're the strategist, yet.

—What about my father, what do I tell him? Maybe we should let my mother explain things to him.

—No . . . please . . . not that . . .

—And what do we tell him?

—I hope he didn't hear you. . . . He's looking sad, all of a sudden, I'm afraid he heard you.

—Well, quick, tell me what to say!

—Tell him the truth . . . he's the only one who should know it.

—What truth?

—Tell him you're afraid . . . tell him that there is real danger tonight, but that the women shouldn't know. Ask him to give you courage, because you'll need it. There's real danger tonight. The police know there will be a meeting somewhere. By now they may have found out where it will take place. You'll be meeting people from an underground organization. You haven't been responsible for any violence yet, but they are. The government wants them, dead or alive. You're frightened, and you need your father's support.

— . . .

—Explain everything to him, and he'll give you what you need, Larry.

—I don't think he'll understand . . . that there's anything other than self-interest . . . worth fighting for . . . that there's any other value . . . worth upholding . . .

—Are you sure?

—Yes.

—Let's see . . . what makes you so sure? What have you seen him do that makes you so sure?

—Everything in the past. He doesn't understand . . . why one would waste time reading a book . . . if it didn't help one to make money. . . . It's stupid and effeminate . . . shows you're a little off. . . . He can be kind and affectionate sometimes, but he'll never understand . . . why you should put yourself in danger . . .

—Larry, please . . . give him one last chance. . . . Simply give me the reasons, and if I'm able to understand them . . . he will, too. . . . Tell me why you've decided to go to that meeting . . . in spite of the terrible danger . . . I'll try to understand, I promise . . .

—There's a great struggle going on all over the world . . . in many locales, and it's waged daily. . . . It's several hundred years old; it determines everything . . . the conditions of our existence, our prospects. . . . It has to be fought. . . . I don't love you all any less, for leaving you now. . . . It's a struggle that includes all of us. . . . We can't distance ourselves from it . . .

—But the people you're associating with, are they trustworthy?

—Some are, and some will crack under the pressure. . . . But the stronger we are, the fewer will crack . . .

—But why you? Couldn't it be somebody old, somebody without a family, somebody with nothing to lose?

—The old need to rest, the young to fight, Mr. Ramirez.

—No, the old want to die, but cannot find an honorable way out . . . I'd only understand your leaving us if you were irreplaceable tonight at the meeting.

—You know I'm irreplaceable, I'm the only one who can work out the strategy, and convince them that it can be done.

—Larry . . . I'm not sure that I've understood . . . I'm not totally convinced . . . I can't think at this moment of any reason that could justify your death. . . . What comes first for your dear ones . . . is that you stay alive. . . . Nothing could be more important . . .

— . . .

—I see I'm disappointing you . . . but I cannot lie to you. . . . Maybe your father will understand . . . and not disappoint you. . . . I wish we were brighter . . . that you could admire us.

—It's not a question of being bright. . . . My father was formed in a different way . . . poverty, a struggle to survive, overrode everything else. To think beyond that was a luxury he couldn't afford. . . . He tried to pass what he learned on to me, but I was brought up under better conditions, and had to fight him for my freedom. . . . Now he's proud of me, but he doesn't understand me.

—Maybe it's not necessary for you to admire him. . . . Please, give him this last chance . . . trust him completely, Larry.

—Why?

—Tell him everything . . . where you're going; who you will see; your fears; trust him completely.

—Completely?

—Yes, put yourself in his hands.

—What for?

—Give him the choice . . . once you're in his hands he'll be able to do with you as he likes . . .

—I don't trust him, he might destroy me. He might crush me.

—What reason could he have to crush you?

—Sometimes he doesn't know what he's doing. He flies off the handle.

—He's nervous, he loses control . . .

—It's not that he's nervous. He'll be sullen and tolerant for a long time . . . then he'll explode, you can never know when. . . . He's nice, but he'll turn on you . . .

— . . .

—One Saturday afternoon my mother was out shopping, and he was left with us kids. . . . We knew we would have an easier time with him, that he didn't know all the rules of the house. He was upstairs and we were in the basement playing. We started to make noise . . . ran up and down the stairs, ran around the living room, bumping into things . . . yelling and screaming, louder and louder. He bore all this quietly, but we wanted to test his patience a little further . . . we ran around his bedroom throwing things. Then suddenly he lashed out . . . it was a cold rage, we were terrified.

—A cold rage?

—Yes, he only let some of it out. Half of it was still bottled up in him. His face turned white, and his eyes became small and hard. He didn't hit us, just told us to stop. We knew if we provoked him any further he would crush us, annihilate us, wipe us off the face of the earth.

—With his bare hands?

—Yes, with his fists.

—Was that what you feared most, his fists?

—Yes, his hands.

—What if you provoked him further?

—He would wring our necks, that was my mother's phrase. Snap our heads off. Smash our heads in, like kids do to their dolls. Break our limbs.

—Would you survive?

—Maybe, but only as a bloody, messed-up sight.

— . . .

—You can take a doll's head in your hand, crush in its forehead and temples. Then you can put one hand around its chest, the other around its head, and twist its body one way and its head the other. It's like wringing a wet towel, snapping its head off. Snap its arms off like twigs. Your hands are big enough to fit around the doll. Split its legs apart . . . the way you split open a chicken, ripping the cartilage, tearing the flesh, then chewing the meat.

—Larry, you have no choice. . . . The workers, they are waiting for you outside; there is no time to waste. . . . But he's locked the door, you must take him aside and talk to him . . . tell him above all how frightened you are of the danger outside . . . not of him . . . and tell him how much you need his support tonight . . .

— . . .

—The room is almost in darkness . . . it's his bedroom upstairs . . . now you give him all the details . . . of your secret plan . . . you put yourself in his hands . . . and he will finally decide what to do. . . . He can either destroy or help you . . . but if you don't dare go upstairs to him . . . you'll never find out . . .

—You understand why I must take this risk at the union hall; he never will; it's beyond him. I don't have any more time, besides, it's too risky telling him. Make up a story, be vague, satisfy him.

—The door is locked.

—I'll bust it open. Distract him while I'm leaving.

—And the window, Larry? You can jump out the window. It wouldn't be the first time.

—Why do you say that?

—Very good . . . don't worry about us anymore . . . go now.

—Now I must go, but I'm frightened.

—You're afraid you may die?

—Yes, that they'll come after me, Mr. Ramirez.

—I'm not afraid, anymore . . . you see? You convinced me, you have to go, it's what you have to do. . . . I'll distract your father while you leave.

—Thank you.

— . . .

—And before I go out to fight I want to tell you that

you've been a great help to me today. What do you feel?

—You mean me?

—Yes, you. Don't you feel satisfied? Where are your sensations?

—Where?

—Yes, where, in your chest, in your throat? You're always bugging me with those questions.

—I'm not feeling anything. I'm warm and comfortable in this bed, and I have no pains . . . but I'm very sleepy; that I must admit. . . . If you don't mind . . . I'd like to doze off for a while . . .

—O.K.

—It's so restful to close your eyes . . . this way. I'll fall asleep very soon. . . . It's good the day's so cloudy. The glare doesn't hurt my eyes, it isn't even necessary to draw the curtains. Just closing my eyes makes it dark and peaceful. . . . I can hear them in the other room; they'll soon open their presents . . . I don't know what Larry's given them; he's already gone and I can't ask him.

—I'm gone and I have important things to do.

—I hope Larry guessed what each of them wanted most as a present, so they'll be pleased, just like me. . . . I won't be able to listen to them any longer because I'm almost asleep.

—My father would like a lot of money, more than anything else. . . . My mother would like a present from him . . . an expensive present, that showed his love for her. My girl friend would be satisfied with a token.

—Larry's father wants a lot of money, but I don't know what he wants to do with it.

—It's nothing in particular he wants, just the power of a lot of money.

—His mother wants an expensive present from his father, what for I don't know.

—She wants something expensive, something luxurious

that would make her beautiful, maybe something she could wear and show off to the other women. Something that would be a symbol of his power, that she could parade around in, not the cheap little presents that he usually gives her.

—And Larry's girl friend, what is the token she'll be satisfied with?

—Anything. She wants Larry most of all. Anything that shows her that he cares for her.

—She's intelligent; she knows he's gone to fight for her, too . . .

—Yes, she doesn't understand much of what he told her, but she knows that it's important, that he's a man of good will. And she's proud of him.

—I can't hear their comments too well; they opened their presents and they're happy with them. Larry's given them exactly what they wanted. He's out in the street now and he knows he has made them all happy. If he were here I'd ask him how it feels.

—He's glad that they're pacified, and that he can return to them.

—Were they pleased with the work you've done?

—Yes, very pleased.

—Say a little more. You're already plunging right into those books. . . . Catch your breath, at least.

—There was a letter from Montreal; they're very pleased with the progress I've made.

—Who did you see at Columbia? The same man who took you to lunch?

—Yes, and he introduced me to some other people in his department.

—Please, look up from those pages. This is becoming intriguing for me; after all, it's me they want to know about.

—Talk to me, I'm listening.

—Before it was magazines; now it's books. Can you read and talk at the same time?

—Yeah, it's only Ford who's incapable of doing two things at once, who can't walk and chew gum at the same time.

—Henry Ford or the President?

—The President. He was always tripping, stepping down from planes, banging his head.

—I really understand what you say better when you're facing me.

—The people in Montreal want me to go there to work.

—Where? Columbia?

—No, Montreal.

—Any reason?

—It makes the paperwork easier for them.

—Bureaucrats.

—Right, bureaucrats.

—But it's out of the question, your parents . . . and your girl friend, although she should have come first—won't permit it.

—All that was fifteen years ago.

—Time couldn't have changed her; she was a marvelous girl; nothing could have spoiled her.

—I haven't seen her in years.

—She won't like your going so far away.

—Hey, look, I don't have anything going with her anymore.

—That's not possible. If that were true . . . that would mean . . . she's miserable now. She took such good care of you. . . . You're worrying me now . . .

—She's been living her own life; she's an entirely different person. She doesn't care about my comings and goings. Once in a while we telephone each other.

—You were mistaken then; you thought she was a certain type and you were wrong.

—No, that's not it at all. People change dramatically in ten years of marriage. They become different people. They need to separate.

—They? Maybe you, but she didn't . . .

—We both needed to separate. She never was as I described her to you.

—When you finish your reading today, you're going right home to her as you do every day, aren't you?

—O.K. She said she wouldn't mind if I went to Montreal.

—Really?

—She knows it's important for my career; she understands. The way she understood that night, when I introduced her to my parents. They'll understand, too.

—You're hiding something from me.

— . . .

—Very well, you say she has changed, but that's your point of view. For some reason I'm convinced she didn't, but I can't prove it. I like her very much and until you can prove the contrary I'll believe she's still the same girl as before.

—You've never met her. All you know about her is what I've told you. And those were my impressions of many years ago. Half what she was and half what I imagined her to be. We weren't discussing a real person. I could have told you anything, and you'd embellish it and latch on to it, as if it were real.

—What time does she usually get home from work?

—A little after I do. She fixes dinner for both of us, sometimes I peel potatoes; we both do the dishes. Dinner is nice, except when I complain about the food, and she gets upset.

—What's wrong with it?

—Sometimes the potatoes are not cooked enough or even if they are they taste bad, because they're rotten potatoes to begin with. We spend a few hours together, sometimes we go for a walk. Aimlessly. We look at things in shop windows, things we can't afford; we have no money left over, we don't talk much during our walks, we're together out of habit. In the evening I would read novels, but when she was around I would feel guilty. It didn't lead anywhere. TV was out; we agreed not to have a set; we didn't want to become like our parents. But we found ourselves arguing more and more—like them. The apartment was very old; it needed a lot of work; I promised to fix it up, to do this and that. I painted a beautiful picture, but didn't fix a thing; she was angry at me for that. I wasn't building a home for us, neither by making money nor by working on the apartment.

— . . .

—In the evening we'd go to bed early to wake up in time for work the next day. There's not much to our lives, it feels like we're trapped. She makes more money than I do, and I hate my job. I don't want to work at all. But I don't know what I want to do. I know I don't want to do what I'm doing, but I have no ambitions. I would like to spend more time with her.

—No ambitions?

—After a year of that I decided to go back to school at night. My wife was very happy, I was finally going to do something with myself. I was happier, too; it gave me something to tackle.

—When are your classes?

—Six to eight. I go right from work. Afterward we have dinner together; then I have to study. It's hard; there's no time for anything. On weekends I have to study, too, to get good grades, so that I can get a scholarship.

—What does she do while you study?

—She's going to school, too; we both study. There's no time for each other, it's as if we lived in the same barracks.

—Is there a maid helping with the housework?

—Don't be ridiculous. Nobody has maids here, only the rich. The wife is the maid.

—What time does she do housework?

—Late at night, before going to bed. The bed was not even made; she had to make it. Clean the bathroom, dust a little, pick up garbage from the floor. Saturday was for chores, the supermarket, the laundry, housecleaning. We did that together. Once in awhile we treated ourselves, and ate out. But not often. I didn't like to take her out. I was afraid she would notice other men and be attracted to them. She was very attractive, and men were attracted to her. Every time we passed a good-looking guy in the street I would watch her eyes, to see if she glanced at him. I was insanely jealous, but I kept it all to myself. I didn't say a word. Rage built up in me.

—What is her favorite restaurant?

—She likes Italian food.

—Is it crowded?

—Yes, it's crowded and humming. There's a guy sitting at a table across from us, with his girl friend. He keeps looking up and staring at my wife, while he's talking to his woman. It bothers me. And I start to glare at him.

—What does he look like? Is he older than you?

—Yes, he's older, maybe in his late thirties. He's bigger and taller, and blond, with regular features, well-dressed. He's obviously interested in my wife, and I can't stand it. It makes me feel shitty, like I shouldn't be with her, like I'm not worthy of her. What's she doing with me anyhow? She should be with him.

—What does his woman look like?

—I can hardly see her; she has her back to us.

—What is the man going to do? Will he stand up and come to your table and talk to your wife?

—No, he'd like to do that, but he won't. My wife turns to see who I'm glaring at. Their eyes meet. She turns away and we continue our conversation. I search her face to see what she's feeling, but I can't tell.

—She's a very innocent girl; somebody should sit at your table and block her view. I sense that man is not a good person.

—She has no direct view; she has to turn around to see him. . . . Yes, it's true, she's innocent, but things stir in her, which she forgets, or represses. Things that would disrupt our relationship. But they're there, and I sense it.

—I cannot come to the restaurant, because I'm sick, but sometimes you meet friends by chance, and your father happens to enter the place. Would you gladly let him sit at your table?

—He's all right; he's not much of a threat now.

—Where are you going to seat him?

—Anywhere.

—No, at a place where he can block that guy's view of your wife.

—Right.

—Is that obnoxious man still looking at her?

—He's brazen; he still is. He's very interested in her, more than the woman he's with. He'd gladly leave her for the excitement of a new woman.

—Your wife has nothing to fear now; there are two men ready to defend her.

—She feels she's saddled with two nebbishes, while there's an alluring stranger over there.

—What does she think he could give her?

—Something new. Adventure. Romance. Sex. Mystery. He must be freer, more powerful.

—Adventure? What kind?

—I don't know. Something new and different, with a person who's not predictable, who can talk, and imagine things freely. Not like me, with my hang-ups and obsessions.

—You mentioned romance, too.

—His conversation is fluid, he knows how to be charming, to endear himself with her. He's self-assured.

—Does he bring her gifts?

—That's hardly important; he doesn't have to. He takes her out to dinner.

—Is somebody looking at her at the restaurant when the man takes her out to dinner?

—She's looking at him, she doesn't notice anyone else.

—And you mentioned sex.

—It will be better, last longer. He won't feel that pressure on his cock to come, and have to restrain himself. It's difficult for him sometimes; just when a woman is starting to achieve her orgasm he shoots. Sabotage. But he feels awful afterward. The other man will have a steel cock, not feel any pressure, not go limp in the middle. Would pump her until she screamed.

—You mentioned mystery as the last element.

—He's not tied to any narrow routine. He doesn't do shit work, leave and return at the same time each day. He's not tired at the end of the day, whining about his personal needs. His imagination is free.

—If she prefers him because she doesn't know him, she'll be disappointed the moment she finds out who he is.

—Why do you say that?

—Once you know somebody, that person becomes predictable, isn't that so? As predictable as you are to her.

—Maybe you're right, but I always imagine the other guy as being superhuman, without my limitations.

—Larry, I see you'd like to be free of limitations, me, too. . . . What would you be like then?

—If I could imagine myself being free, I'd have no problems, don't you understand?

—Don't worry, you're studying hard enough to get those good grades; you'll be given the scholarship you applied for.

—Yes, it was better when we were both studying. We were freer; we exchanged ideas, played, went to movies.

—No more shit work, as you called it?

—Yes, I was finally free of that. It was wonderful to be a student for years. We used to roll around in bed in the morning, kissing and wrestling. Usually, if it was a weekday morning we wouldn't make love. We saved it for the night, and just hinted at what we might do. Should we save it for later? It's tempting, but classes start at ten, and it's eight-thirty already, and I have to eat and read an article. Just one more tumble; we often felt like it, and I would tease her, lick her. But I had to save some energy for the day's studies. I tease her by sticking it in a little. But then I get dressed, stuffing my erection into my pants; I have to watch out for the zipper. We would never get started otherwise.

— . . .

—We'd have a late breakfast together before we went off to school.

—What was served for breakfast?

—Eggs, toast, juice, cereal, whatever we wanted.

—Does she cook breakfast?

—We took turns doing it.

—Today it's her turn.

—She would cook breakfast just wearing only her panties, scramble some eggs, fix a fresh pot of coffee. Set the table with napkins, butter, jam, juice. Turn on the radio, gabbing away. She'd pop some bread in the toaster, water the plants, light a cigarette. I watch her breasts when she leans over to get milk out of the refrigerator. Pour the coffee, steaming hot. I would snuggle up against her as she served me eggs. She serves herself and we eat and talk. We're glad we didn't make love and saved it for tonight.

—Do you study on your way to class?

—Yeah, on the subway.

—Do you have a good memory? Can you remember what you read easily?

—I store everything like a computer. My brain categorizes and relates the material; it's easy for me. I get good grades.

—What do your professors say?

—I'm the favorite of a few of them. Especially those in my own field, they see a bright future for me. It hasn't yet materialized, has it?

—Are the other students jealous of you?

—Probably, but I pay them no attention. I don't need them. I have my professors and my wife, that's all I need. They have faith in me. They lift my spirits.

—Any particular subject that you prefer?

—It was later in grad school that I got interested in Marxism, after studying history for umpteen years. All the facts seemed to fall into place. Finally, a theory that accounted for the resentment and rebelliousness we felt toward our society.

— . . .

—It was exhilarating, liberating. I plunged eagerly into my studies. It was as if a confused, inarticulate part of me was given a language and permitted to speak. It's still very much within me.

—Where is it located? Is it in your lungs? Inside your skull? In your throat?

—What kind of question is that?

—Is it in your hands?

—In my knees and my elbows! What stupidity! You don't make sense.

— . . .

—Well, if you want an answer, it's in my head and hands.

— . . .

—It's still very much a part of me, awaiting the proper time and conditions to reemerge. . . . After being swamped by ideology since childhood. Newspapers, television, political campaigns, advertising, churches, schools, always vaguely detesting them, but having no coherent response.

Turning away in disgust toward literature, refinement, some cultural ballast for the pack of lies, the platitudes. Marxism seemed to provide the answer to how to maintain one's integrity and engage, instead of fleeing, social reality.

—Did you learn it in a course?

—I had a teacher in graduate school, a total obscurantist, into German philosophy, who used Marx to illustrate various methodological principles. But anyhow, we had to read him and that was enough to turn us on.

—Did he dislike Marx?

—No, he liked him; but he thought there were some things that he understood better than Marx. Anyhow, I'm grateful to that guy for turning me on to Marx. I was in a political group for a while, a Marxist group, but they're impossible in this country. Completely detached from any social base. Their arguments, in-fighting, maneuvering, invective, personality clashes, were more than I could stand. I had to leave.

—Were they terrorists?

—No, just toward other members.

—Detached from any social base?

—Endless discussions of the working class, but not a worker in the group. Arguments so Byzantine and doctrinaire, they couldn't engage the interest of any worker.

—You could have enlisted your father.

—He's the last person in the world who would have been interested. He wanted to escape from the working class, own his own business.

— . . .

—There's a particular danger involved in Marxism, for young people. Aside from the moral coherence and the voice it gives to so many feelings and sentiments. It's such a total critique of society, and the mission it sets itself so overshadows other concerns that young people who embrace Marxism often find within it the means to deny the

necessity for any further exploration of their own psyche.
— . . .

—Marxism claims that the survival of the human species depends on the overthrow of capitalist social relations, that the system tends to be more and more destructive. What higher moral task could there be? . . . There were some personal difficulties that I managed to postpone wh?~ I plunged into Marxism. My difficulties with women, sexual problems, my difficulties in getting a job, in being really aggressive about my own career and economic situation, as opposed to abstractly aggressive about the overthrow of society . . . it enabled me to remain really passive by accepting an ostensibly active and aggressive set of ideas.

—Who gets home first, you or your wife?

—It depends on the night; we get home at different hours. But we know the other is coming soon. We were like two kids, playmates. Inseparable.

—Did you ever see the man in the restaurant again?

—No, but there were many others.

—She's not looking at them, she can't, the view is blocked.

—You're right, she didn't. But I didn't know it at the time. I invented difficulties.

—But now you know. And she doesn't want you to go to Montreal. She's afraid something may happen to you, if you're left all alone.

—Do you want to come, too?

—Where?

—Montreal.

—I don't want to be a burden. . . . But maybe, who knows . . . maybe I could be of some help there.

—Maybe . . .

—If my health improves I'm sure I'll be able to remember more. They insist it's all psychological, but I believe it's physical; it's my blood: it doesn't reach my brain properly.

Getting stronger would change everything for me.

—What a cunt you are.

—That's pretty strong language.

—You whine and whine, but you're tough as nails.

—Larry, how about going back to your books and leaving me in peace for a while?

—Good idea.

—This young man thinks we old people are fools. What an error in judgment! As if a long life weren't the best teacher. He thinks I haven't realized anything. All right . . . if I weren't so weary I'd get up and pull the curtains and look at the nocturnal snow falling on this Muscovite square.

—This old codger is so absentminded, he doesn't see a thing. I'm always using his own paper to run off subversive leaflets on his own printing press, while all he thinks about is taking medicines for his cold.

—What a beautiful square; the temple's gilded towers shine with hope even at night. The moon over the Moskova river; could its gleam be an accomplice to the Czar's henchmen? This foolhardy lad is distributing leaflets God knows where, yes, the teachers are on a hunger strike inside the school, they've locked themselves up there, protesting notorious crimes.

—I can't cover up my footsteps in the snow; if the police felt like following me they'd find me in no time. But I've got to get to the building next to the school, climb the wall and shower tokens of solidarity from the rooftop. The voice of every enslaved Russian will reach their ears if I could only scale these slippery tiles.

—A Czarist patrol. No matter how much the snow muffles the clank of their boots, I can smell these vultures, carrion hanging from their hooded beaks; they don't use napkins at their funereal feasts.

—This old codger is so absentminded, he doesn't see a

thing. The girl who lives with him has aquiline features, high cheekbones, a thin nose, a well-sculpted head.

—The little girl that lives in my house is very tall and stately for her age.

—Her little-girl clothes still show what a good figure she has. Her clothes are modest, not sexy at all.

—The child who lives in my house is a very serious little girl.

—Her modesty makes her even more attractive. The old guy doesn't know that we're secretly engaged. We're keeping it from him 'cause we're afraid that he'll take it badly and fire me. And that would be fatal for a poor peasant like me.

—The little girl is in love with that pauper. I realized it long ago. An immature lad if there ever was one, but deep down he's not bad. Anyway, I know him like the palm of my hand; he's better than a total stranger. What's more, we men are all like that, a bundle of defects, egotistical and stubborn, cunning; the poor thing won't have much to choose from.

—A few more cautious steps over this gable and I'll be looking down on the vast schoolyard, and there they go, gliding through the air, leaflets full of hope.

—Shots in the distance! Those accursed vultures have met up with some popular-resistance group. Maybe a whole patrol hunting one man, who happens to be a bundle of defects, egotistical and stubborn, cunning, immature, but not so bad deep down.

—Damn snow, my footprints are giving me away; all the doors are slamming shut, I hear it louder and louder, the screeching of those horrible predators. In a few minutes they'll be on top of me.

—The henchmen are approaching this part of the city; there's no doubt it's him they are after. What amazes me is that he would dare ask me to hide him. He could get in through this open door. One more minute of delay and the

Czarists won't know which door in the alley he disappeared through.

—Thank you, sir! . . . It may seem strange to you . . . that I'm so out of breath . . . but I was being chased . . . by a band of thieves . . .

—I know very well what kind of thieves were chasing you, that's why I waited here with the door open, don't treat me like a fool.

—A knock! It's them!

—Don't worry, I'll protect you. . . . Come in, defenders of the order! Yes, I know very well what you're looking for; the wretch is waiting for you. He took advantage of my naiveté to cover up his illegal doings. But you have him now, and you can take him away. Thanks for taking out yesterday's garbage for me. . . . But first, if you will allow me . . . I'd like to thank you for your kindness with a good strong drink, the finest spirits in our empire of snow and ice. . . . That's the way, down the hatch, there's a lot more where that came from! . . . That's it, another . . . yes! Of course you can have another one! That'll warm your innards, bottoms up! . . . And now just another, to warm the cockles of your hearts . . . and another!

—But . . . sir . . . you saved me. . . . They're falling like drunken bears . . .

—Don't insult the animal kingdom. There's no time to lose, get the sled ready while I look for the child. We must escape, and I know you wouldn't leave without her.

—Sir . . . I've misjudged you . . .

—She's asleep. When I lifted her in my arms she didn't wake up. Fear keeps her large eyes from opening; I'm familiar with the tricks of hearts besieged by adversity. Climb into the driver's seat, and let's get going, every moment counts.

—Sir . . . the driver is the one who knows the way. I don't know where to go.

—You're cunning; I knew that already. You just want to

sit next to her. But I won't permit it; I'll show you the way from my place.

—As you wish, sir.

—You're crying, lad, I'm hearing your voice break for the second time.

—Out of gratitude, sir, you saved my life, by putting yours and the girl's in danger.

—Her life and yours are irrevocably bound together, whatever happens to you and me happens to her also.

—Thank you . . . sir . . .

—Hold your tears, man. Follow the example of these dogs; they do their duty without a word . . . look how they find their way through these endless steppes. . . . And now that I think of it, well, why not? You get in back and I'll take the reins for a while. But hold her tightly, take care of her for me, though I know that won't be a problem for you.

—Thank you . . . sir, you worked very hard at your profession, didn't you? You must have been very diligent, painstaking, patient. Evidently you had an academic background like me. And you acquired your work habits painfully. But there came a point when you loved to work, when it was no longer painful, when dealing with books and abstractions and subjects divorced from daily life became pleasurable and comfortable, wasn't that so?

—I guess you're right. But what's wrong with that?

—Nothing, but good things can be dangerous, seductive. Because of your accomplishments, and because you do socially productive work, your mind can legitimately unburden itself of other tasks that may be painful or difficult.

—Such as what?

—You sacrifice your family for the sake of your job.

—Is that true of me?

—You're the living example of the opposite.

—Thank you . . . but it took an awful lot to convince you.

—No, not at all . . . it is I who should thank you . . . kind sir . . .

—I think I can hear those Czarist butchers approaching, hold her tight, I'll whip the dogs to go faster.

—I'll watch over her, don't worry. And when your hands are sore from holding the reins I'll take your place. That's what happens among friends.

—Damn snow, the sled marks are giving us away. The henchmen are behind us.

—Yes, sir, don't you think they are accursed vultures?

—Yes, horrible predators.

—Sir, and don't you think there's carrion hanging from their hooked beaks, since they don't use napkins at their funereal feasts?

—Those were my very words. Lad, we agree on just about everything, I see, too bad that the enemy is now hot on our trail and there's so little time to chat.

—Sir . . . sir! I'm frightened . . . there's real danger tonight, I need the support . . . of somebody. . . . Sir . . . they're firing at us . . .

—Duck, don't give them a target.

—Sir . . . they wounded all the dogs . . . they're bleeding to death!

—Yes . . . poor little animals, why should they always be the ones to die? . . . They were with us to the last moment . . .

—Sir, the Czarists have veered off; they must have thought we were dead. They're heading south.

—And we'll keep to the north, where it gets colder and colder.

—Sir . . . the dogs are behind us dyeing the snow red, soon the tempest will cover them with its immaculate mantle . . . but how is it that we keep advancing? I can't figure it out . . . in this white turbulence I can't see beyond my nose.

—We're advancing slowly, but we're advancing. I'm the one who's pulling the sled, while I have the strength.

—You? How is it possible . . . you're an old man who's always sick . . .

—In a few moments, when I've lost all my strength
. . . you can take my place . . .

—Sir, will I have the strength to pull the sled?

—You certainly will . . .

—Sir, several white landscapes are already behind us, let
me take your place. . . . But on one condition, that you give
this little girl all your devoted care, that you don't forget to
watch over her for a single second.

—Do you dare tell me how to watch over her, something
I've been doing for her whole life?

—Sir, have you known her for that long? I thought you'd
never seen her before.

—Oh, the fool. I've taken care of her since she was born!

—Why, since she's not your daughter?

—Never mind that. Would you allow me to take care of
you and the girl, as I have been doing up to now?

—I'll have to think about that, sir.

—I'm . . . I'm . . . begging . . . you to . . .

—Sir, you're out of breath . . .

—Lad, why are we taking this route? I really don't know
why we're following the north star.

—Sir . . . it's the only way out of the Czarist realm, the
only way to save her.

—Tell me when you're tired; I'm holding her in my arms,
and for some reason it's as if I'm seeing her for the first time.

—You're really seeing her for the first time; admit it and
forget your stupid pride.

— . . .

—Admit it, sir.

— . . .

—Silence means yes, according to an old proverb.

—As long as she doesn't realize, I don't mind admitting
it. She's sleeping, she can't hear. In a little while we'll be out
of danger.

—Sir, don't waste your breath talking, soon you'll have to take your turn.

—And the same goes for you, don't waste your breath talking, until we're really out of danger.

—Is it very cold outside?

—Yes, freezing.

—I look terrible, don't I?

—No worse than usual.

—Well, today I have bad news.

—Keep it to yourself.

—I'm afraid it affects you, too. The doctor in charge of this ward told me it was out of the question for me . . . to travel.

—How does that affect me?

—They don't think I should go back to the home; they say New York is already too cold for me. Montreal would be impossible.

—I don't know what to say.

—He's not my personal doctor, though. I only trust the one the committee assigned to me.

—Have you talked to him recently?

—Well, he came last week. He was the one who insisted on my staying here one week more.

—How do you feel about that? What do you want to do?

—The hospital depresses me. It's obvious my health is not improving; I blame it all on this damn place. The minute I leave I'll feel much better.

—Where do you want to go?

—Montreal, where else? . . . Are you already starting to read again?

—Yes, there's a lot of work still to be done.

—What day of the week is it?

—Friday.

—You're being paid for today; you're supposed to wheel me around three times a week.

—Do you feel well enough to go out?

—Not really . . . not if it's freezing. The doctor's forbidden it. What's more, I am going to be extremely careful, so I can travel soon. . . . You know, staying here has weakened me terribly. When the male nurse takes me to the bathroom I get dizzy . . . and dizzier. No improvement, and it's all the fault of this place.

—So what do you want to talk about?

—Tell me what she fixed you for breakfast today.

—Why? Are you hungry?

—I wasn't able to touch the lunch tray. That stupid doctor ruined my appetite with his nonsense this morning. But now, yes, I'd feel like having a bite to eat; only I can't make up my mind about what to order.

— . . .

—Why should these people in Montreal get us all in trouble? I don't see the need for us to go all the way up there, you, your wife and I.

—You're right; but they're supporting the project, and they set the conditions.

—Your job could be done right down here.

—But they won't pay for it.

—What if your wife really says she won't stand being left alone? And what if I'm not allowed to travel north?

—I've told you I haven't lived with her for years. If you don't want me to go just say so. There is no need to drag in fictitious characters. Tell me about your own feelings. We can't talk otherwise.

—All I hope is that she's not dead.

—She's perfectly healthy, and lives alone. If she were dead she'd have no complaints about my going to Montreal. It's you who doesn't want me to go. Why? We'd both benefit.

—You told me you got your scholarship; I don't see what the problem is, then. You promised to tell me all about the breakfast she served you today.

—I'd like a little respect for my life. Not how it was, or how you would like it to be, to suit your own needs, which I don't understand. But respect for my life as it is.

—Respect?

—Forget about respect; just acknowledge reality. I've been divorced for five years.

—You told me all your problems were solved when the scholarship arrived, and I believed you. Now you want me to believe the opposite, and I can't.

—So don't.

—O.K., you've tested my patience long enough; stop joking and tell me about breakfast.

—I had a glass of orange juice and a yogurt. What did you have?

—I don't remember. All I remember is I couldn't eat lunch after the doctor's stupid comments.

— . . .

—The lack of nourishment is weakening me; I must order some lunch even if it's late. Of course, your telling me what she cooked last night will whet my appetite.

—What do you feel like eating?

—Only what she cooked for you last night.

—Then you're not really hungry.

—I need to see her again, soon. . . . Nothing would be more painful to me than to stop seeing her . . . ever again . . .

—What are you talking about? You've never seen her.

—Maybe it would have been better if I hadn't. Now I need to see her again, and to hear her, make sure that she's there. Soon the studies will be over, and although I know you like this college life, there will be even better things for you and her.

—No, it was more difficult when our studies ended. Students' life is part imaginary; you live in different centuries, in different parts of the globe; it gives free rein to and rewards fantasy. When we started to work it was different, reality set in. It was a teaching job that consumed a lot of time. Preparations at night and over the weekend; a job that paid a pretty small salary.

—Was it enjoyable?

—Yes. But I put extra pressures on myself to do a super job, and that made it difficult.

—Extra pressures?

—Yes, I had to please all the students, and be admired by all the faculty. Somehow my identity was tied up with that. I had to shine and be the star. It's funny how we set ourselves certain goals. I had a beautiful wife and smarts. There was no need for it.

—So again you had to work after dinner.

—Yes, I gave myself extra work.

—There are potatoes on the table; are they well-cooked tonight?

—Yes, they're fine, but we're starting to have disagreements.

—Slight ones, nothing more.

—I was happy with my job, and plunged deeper and deeper into my work. During every spare minute I would read and take notes. My studies were endless, from Marx back to Hegel, from Hegel to German idealism. A world of riches opened up. I was completely absorbed. My wife didn't like it. "I feel I'm competing with Marx and Hegel," she said. There is no reason for two people ever to get bored with each other. How can you exhaust another human being? The things you find out about each other, how could it ever get boring? But it was. Just the two of us in that big apartment, no kids, just cats. Books and papers. Sometimes sex was the only comforting thing. After an evening working separately, more interest in the books than in each other, we would go to bed mechanically, out of boredom, and it would be good and soothing; but that's all there was, and

that became boring. I wanted a new woman in my life. Or
at least I thought I did. I had fantasies about every woman
I saw. My fantasy life mushroomed. I was attracted to the
woman upstairs. When I was alone I would masturbate and
think of her.

—What does she tell you, the woman upstairs?

—She's a housewife; I turned her on to Marxism. She
spends part of her day reading economics and philosophy.
She gets very excited about it. We have long discussions; we
warm up to each other.

—Yes . . .

—She's bored with her husband, too. We find each other
exciting. Sometimes she comes down to talk when my wife's
not home. I fix her tea, and we enjoy those moments. I'm
more and more drawn to her. She seems more and more
loving. But her kid takes too much of her time. We need to
be alone, to make love. I'd like to switch wives.

—Did her husband suspect anything?

—No, he was too stupid.

—Your wife wouldn't have liked him.

—She started going out with other men. On the sly. But
left enough evidence so that I would suspect something. She
tried to provoke me into paying attention to her. Into loving
her again. She got further and further out of hand.

—What do you have to study after dinner, tonight?

—We're getting further and further apart. There's no
stopping it now. It's unbearably empty living with each
other. Things are going to explode.

—Are you liked by all the students? Are you admired by
all the faculty?

—Some of them like me and some of them hate what I'm
doing. It's a Catholic college. I have enemies there. The
administration is trying to get rid of me. It's a bullshit college anyhow; I should be looking for a better job, but I'm
not. I'm hanging in there enjoying my work. I have to start
working on my Ph.D., but I'm not interested. I should be

getting involved in projects, to make money, to meet people who would help me. But I'm not interested in that either. My wife is very disappointed in me; she wants me to hustle, build a career for myself. She wants a house in the country, a car, nice vacations, travel and leisure, that she expects me to provide, so that her life will have meaning.

—She doesn't have a child, like the woman upstairs?

—Yes, she would like a child very much. But I don't make enough money. And I'm deathly afraid of one. It would rob me of my freedom. She gets pregnant and aborts spontaneously. She feels terrible. She's depressed. But I'm relieved. She gets pregnant again, this time I tell her it's O.K., we can have the baby, we'll make out somehow, she can stop working, I'll pick up another job. She's very happy; it's what she wants. But she aborts again. And I'm relieved.

—You say you're enjoying your work.

—Yes, I like preparing lectures, organizing them, polishing them, feeling that my skills are improving. And being good for the students that way. And learning something myself, making new finds.

—Do hours go by quickly when you're preparing lectures?

—Yes, and my energy level is high. It was the discovery that I could see things that others didn't. That my mind had something to offer. Work gave me a sense of importance, of individuality, of reality. Whatever else I didn't know or couldn't do, I could do this. Yes, my wife was nice to have around, she was auxiliary, I thought. I devoted less time to her, and more to my work. . . . I preferred working and growing to hustling and career building. That was best, I feel. I made the right choice.

—Was working like that a means to something or an end in itself?

—An end in itself, of course. It was the only time in my life that I felt that way.

— . . .

—You're supposed to go after jobs for the money and the possibilities of advancement. If you find one that's meaningful in itself, so much the better. But it's not the primary thing you go after. Mine was really a shitty job. I should have used it as a stepping-stone in my career, instead of as an end in itself. The faculty members who intended to stay there, and were comfortable, were considered failures, deadwood.

—Maybe they were enjoying their work; why shouldn't they have stayed?

—They weren't deeply into what they were doing. It was just the security of the job that attracted them. For those who were alive or in transition, their jobs were a means to further their careers, to marshal and consolidate their forces, make contacts, start building bridges to future jobs. If you weren't doing that, you were considered hopeless; talented ambitious people had to be on the move.

—Your work was meaningful in itself; it gave you pleasure. Did you feel bad about that?

—No, of course not. It was my main source of happiness; I embraced it to avoid dealing with my wife, and the growing tension between us, the demands she was starting to make. Things got really bad when her father died. Her mourning wasn't normal; it was something more; she was very fond of him, but at the same time disappointed in him. Disappointed that he never became what he could have been. Never got out of the working class. As much as she loved him she was deeply disappointed in him; he didn't live up to her expectations. And when he died she was really torn; she started to drink, heavily. To ease the pain. She became very dissatisfied with me. She was always complaining about what I didn't give her, and that I was stingy with my time and affection.

—You're lying either to me or to yourself. If that job satisfied you so much, why did you refuse the chance to return to your field a few days ago?

—I was satisfied with my job; I'm not lying.

—I don't believe you.

—Yes, it was fulfilling; and maybe that was wrong, the fact that it reflected self-absorption, personal gratification, without transcendence.

—What kind of transcendence?

—A way out of me, out of that zone where everything rots.

—Where does she hide when she wants to drink?

—How did you know she hid?

—She's ashamed; she has to hide.

—Yes, and she knew I would disapprove.

—Where does she hide?

—I never knew. When I balanced the checkbook I saw that there were a lot of checks made out to the liquor store. She said it was where she got cash. I believed her.

—Where are the bottles?

—Hidden under the sink. Gallon bottles of cheap wine, and Scotch, and vodka. They were hidden behind the detergents. She drank late at night, sometimes after I went to sleep, sometimes about an hour before. It was sort of O.K. to drink then, after work, after dinner, after preparing her lessons; she was also teaching. It was reasonable to have a glass of wine, to relax before going to bed. I would go to bed first, lie in bed, waiting for her to come, because I wanted to make love. She would come . . . maybe forty-five minutes later, drunk, in her nightie, with her legs—as thick and strong as they were—wobbling, and she'd fall into bed, smelling of Scotch. Her eyes were glazed and vacant, but usually she wanted to be held, and I would fuck her because I thought it was sexy to fuck a drunk. Sometimes she would take another swig of Scotch, before sucking my cock. And I loved it because it felt so cool. She'd be so drunk it was an effort for her to take off her nightie, and I would lie her down, put her limp legs on my shoulders, and fuck her mercilessly. All those difficulties during the evening, all the complaints, dissatisfactions, when all I wanted was peace when I came home. Peace and satisfaction. Finally I had her in a position where I could get something out of her. And I took my fill, still resentful . . . at the troubles she had caused me. . . . So it was loveless, sadistic. Do you know that people can make love with the intent to punish? That would happen periodically, throughout our marriage. Resentments would build up, which weren't expressed, for whatever reason. And sometimes the lovemaking would be an act of hate, orgasm and all. Pure hate. Vengeance. Nothing was said, but you knew it. After, as I'd fall asleep, I would hear her get up again, and go for more booze. She had insomnia. God knows how long it took her to knock herself out.

—I'm not feeling well. There seems to be no air in this room. Please open the window.

—You're going to feel worse. She started to see other men on the sly. It was a long time before I suspected anything. Even with the drunkenness and the resentments and the coldness between us, we still trusted each other. After ten years of living together a certain confidence develops, so I dismissed all the obvious clues . . . all the evidence that she was having affairs. One night I went to bed; it was a cool summer night. She had not yet come home; it was very late. I climbed into our double bed, alone, and tried to fall asleep. I couldn't. I just lay there, waiting for her footsteps up the stairs . . . and the key in the lock. Nothing. . . . At four o'clock I heard a car pull up in front of the house. I heard her get out, and say something to somebody. When she came in I was furious; I turned on the lights and started screaming. "Where have you been? Why didn't you call?" She said she met some ex-priest, and they started reminiscing, about his religious phase and this and that. The conversation had been so engrossing they lost track of time. I was very suspicious, to say the least. And I was still angry, but she insisted that's what had happened, and I believed her.

We didn't lie to each other after all those years. Finally, it was the woman upstairs who told me that my wife was seeing other men.

—It gets too cold with the window open.

—It's going to get colder. The woman upstairs is my friend, my wife's friend also; they're very close. But she tells me anyway, and she's very broken up and disturbed by it. Her loyalties are torn. When I listen to her I feel so cold; I know it's the end. There have been a half-dozen affairs; she's trying out men like gloves, women even. I know it's the end of our relationship. I don't trust her anymore. I think that hurts the most.

—I shouldn't have asked you to open the window. I feel my chest constricting.

—She was getting drunk earlier and earlier in the evening, eight o'clock, six o'clock. Her needs were great and pressing; but she didn't know what they were. She would interrupt me when I was studying, drunk, "Larry, why don't we talk, we never talk anymore, you never talk about your feelings." . . . Her field was English literature. I felt only . . . rage . . . which I didn't express. I should have left her then, but I couldn't budge, as horrible as the situation was; I wanted to force it back into the old mold, "I'll talk later . . . I'm working now." She couldn't hear; she was drunk, and in great pain. She needed me, and I probably could have given more than I did. But it's very difficult, impossible, to deal with an alcoholic. Perhaps there was nothing I could have done. . . . Anyhow, she kept doing things that disturbed my routine. And my routine became more and more rigid. I drew farther and farther away from her. But she did more and more to provoke me.

— . . .

— . . .

—Yes . . .

—She would continue babbling when I read. There was

no place in the apartment where I could go. I would watch TV for a half-hour before going to bed; she would turn it off and insist on talking. I would turn it on again. She would turn it off. Once she tried to stop me from turning it back on and I pushed her out of the way. We started to fight; she called the police, claiming I had beaten her. I was mortified and frustrated. I kept pouring gallons of wine down the drain, but she always found a way. I began to hate her, but I couldn't detach myself. She started a new tactic. She told me to leave. I couldn't; I said, "You leave." She couldn't, at least not yet, and not alone. I believe she wanted something major from me. Something connected to her father's death. But neither of us knew what it was; and we fought. One night she had a friend over for dinner, a young guy, a friend of her brother's. . . . I didn't mind, although he wasn't particularly interesting, but anyhow after dinner they were both high and talking. I got bored with the conversation, so I went to bed. She said she'd be in shortly. I went to bed but couldn't fall asleep, kept hearing their chatter. It seemed to go on for hours. And then suddenly there was silence. I didn't hear him leave. Instead there was rustling. I froze, became all ears. It was pitch black in the apartment, but I could hear everything. They were lying down on the couch, kissing and petting. I could have gotten up, and thrown him out in a rage . . . as was my right. . . . Instead I was terror-struck and excited . . . waiting for the inevitable to happen. Finally he penetrated her, and I heard her sob "Yes." My feelings were so confused, I couldn't get out of bed; all I could do was listen . . . "Now I can do it whenever I want," she said. "Yes, isn't it better that way?" he said. It had finally happened; she was free of me. I had expected this from the very beginning. But to hear her moan, in another man's arms, was most exciting. I can't explain why, but to be an outsider, a listener, an eavesdropper . . .

— . . .

— . . . to hear her sexual response from a distance, in the dark, in another room, with another man, why was that more exciting than to hear her moan when she was with me? My feelings were torn . . . I also suffered from an inferiority complex that caused me great pain. It was as if I always knew that another man would satisfy her more sexually. And it finally happened, and my fascination with hearing her being turned on by another man, it's my father fucking my mother, it's my fascination with hearing my mother moan.

— . . .

—The guy was a schmuck. A skinny hippie, homely, with a big mop of hair, a lightweight . . . frivolous . . . a product of his time . . . while she was as big as I, robust, athletic . . . the whole thing made no sense.

—You couldn't miss the chance to bring in that mother business. At the least opportunity you bring it up. As if you thought it would please me. It disgusts me, because it isn't true. You tell that story to cover up for something much worse.

—I don't know how to respond to that.

—Maybe it's better to feel shame than to feel nothing at all. Maybe you're not capable of feeling anything else. And that frightens you even more.

—Listen, you said you had nothing to eat, can I order you something now?

—No, I'm not hungry. I'm not hungry at all.

—Come in.

—Hi! How are you feeling?

—The same, I guess. . . . How is it outside?

—It's cold, but it feels good.

—You're looking into my eyes, Larry, what's the matter?

—Nothing's the matter; the trip's all arranged. I spent a couple of hours at Columbia working out the details; I was there all morning. We were supposed to have lunch there, but there were too many preparations still unmade. He had a class at two; there was no time.

—He? Who is he?

—The man at Columbia. I grabbed something to eat on my way downtown.

—Oh yes? What did you have?

—I stopped at a Cuban-Chinese restaurant. I felt like treating myself a little. I had a big plate of chicken and rice and beans.

—So the trip's all arranged?

—Yes, everything's taken care of.

—The committee doctor was here this morning, finally.

—What did he say?

—He said I could go to Montreal . . . you might have guessed it, since you told the university people that I was coming along.

—Terrific, that's great. I'm glad you're feeling better.

—But what if the doctor had said no? Didn't you rush things a bit? Did you really tell them I was coming, too?

—I said you might be coming, depending on how you felt.

—But what if I hadn't been able to go? Would they have continued the project, anyhow?

—Well, yes . . .

—I see . . .

— . . .

—It's Thursday; you're not paid to come today. What are you doing here?

—I'm here to work on your books, as usual.

—I see . . .

—Let me wash this greasy taste out of my mouth; let me use your sink.

—Go ahead.

—Let me wash my hands, too; I ate the chicken with my hands.

—And that magazine you have in your greasy hand, you picked it out of the garbage.

—No, I indulged myself and bought it.

—I couldn't eat lunch today, again.

—Why not? You've plenty of free time here.

—Bad news killed my appetite.

—Uh oh . . . what news? Be gentle with me.

—I'll try . . . the doctor from the committee was here.

—Yeah? You've already told me.

—He examined me.

—Yes . . . so?

—He did because I insisted so much. He had already told me over the phone that I shouldn't go to a colder climate. And he was preparing to transfer me to a much better home, so they say, in Palm Springs. To a dry, warm desert climate.

—What are you talking about? You just said you were going to Montreal.

—It was a bad joke, I'm sorry.

—I don't know what to believe anymore.

—Why should you care? You've gone ahead and made arrangements with Columbia without knowing whether I could come along.

—I was hoping you'd be able to.

—Me, too. But now it's evident that I'm not.

—That's a shame, I'm really sorry, Mr. Ramirez.

—What are you planning to do in that case?

—I'd still like to go to Montreal.

—I see . . .

— . . .

—I'm not going to Palm Springs. I want to stay here. Everything's going to be all right . . . if I can count on your assistance, of course.

—But Palm Springs would suit you.

—Nonsense, you can be warm in any New York room; it's just a matter of regulating the heating.

—What are you going to do here?

—I'm all right here; why move to California or Montreal?

—But Montreal would be good for me, Mr. Ramirez.

—Don't rush things. I'm only asking for a little of your time.

—That's absurd. You can't expect such a sacrifice.

—Come on, don't be a child. A little discipline, please. I'm going to stay here, forget about Palm Springs, so you can keep coming to work on the books. I'm sure I'll get better.

—I think you should go to Palm Springs, they say it's beautiful. The sun and the dryness will be good for your health.

—But it would be impossible for you to come along; the expenses would be enormous. The most important thing is that you keep working here on the books. You might make some interesting finds.

—I wouldn't expect to go with you to Palm Springs. And, anyway, I have to take the books with me to Canada.

—That means you accept the idea of going alone to Montreal.

—Yes, though I'd prefer you to come with me.

—Larry, first put that magazine down; look at me.

— . . .

—Larry, no more childish mischief; don't make me so nervous. You're trying to frighten me, as you have so many other times, and then laugh at me. But this is not the right time. You just made a silly joke, right?

—What joke?

—Look at me when you talk to me!

—Mr. Ramirez, you're overdoing it. I'm not joking. There is interesting work for me in Montreal, and a perfect place for your health in Palm Springs.

—You astonish me . . .

—Why?

—I never thought you would be so ungrateful.

—What do you mean?

—I mean ungrateful. I took you into my confidence . . . and all you can think of is making a quick profit off me.

—I was afraid that you might react badly. But you'll benefit from this project also. Your contributions and a little more of the history of your country . . . will be known. . . . Yes, it's also important for me personally; the contacts, some money, and most important, a chance for me to work at my profession. What's wrong with all that?

—I see what you are, a greedy materialistic caricature of an American, all you can think of is profits.

—What profits? I'll be getting a salary. As a labor organizer you should know the difference between profits and wages.

—You're trying to confuse me with words.

—No, you're angry at me and I don't understand why.

—I'm disappointed . . . in you. And angry with myself for having expected more from you. I expected sympathy, even friendship . . . but that's something you evidently cannot give.

—Haven't I been your friend?

—Now I see you haven't.

—Why don't you want me to leave?

—Now I wouldn't want to go to Montreal with you. Now that I know what you are.

—You're being completely unreasonable. Everybody

would profit from this project . . . I've tried to treat you as an adult, to talk to that part of you, the healthy part. Your survival depends on the strength of that part. But you keep slipping back. Your paranoia means death.

—Those shrinks have taught you a few words, haven't they? But they don't impress me. . . . They just can't wait to come to their obvious conclusions. . . . They think it's so easy to find solutions . . . but it takes intelligence, hard work . . . to discover truth. They lack the capacity; they don't work hard enough, they are mediocre . . . you are mediocre . . .

—And you're disgusting.

—Larry, I don't quite understand why you refused to go back to teaching, and now you accept this offer; maybe it's because you would be harming me. I don't know; I'm baffled. But on the other hand, what a relief to see how low you can get! At least I can see that clearly. And what a relief to know that there is nothing to defend, that there is nobody decent to save.

—I never said anything to the contrary.

—And what a relief to know that I do not want to go anywhere with you; and how nice to know that your mother threw you out and is now resting in peace at last! Aahh . . . aahh . . . relief brings out these big sighs; they are released from my very entrails; I'm so glad my diaphragm comes up to my throat. And those blessed students at that third-rate college in Brooklyn, now they are rid of your poisonous classes, and blessed lungs of mine, full of air at last, aahh! Aahh! My ribs hurt; they're too delicate for deep, joyous breathing, this deep satisfaction . . . and your father, he's such a good carpenter! He knew how to saw that two-by-four. Ah, ah, I'm not used to feeling so good . . . I'm hearing so distinctly how well he handles the saw.

—And I'm hearing a madman's ravings.

—I'm crazy with joy; I can't cope with so much satisfaction and relief.

—You're disgusting; I've already told you. I shouldn't try to deal with you anymore . . . but I've been working on your notes and now I know something else about you. You've made those same accusations before. To somebody else.

—What are you insinuating?

—You're impossible. You're living a lie, like a horse with blinders. You won't face up to anything, not the least bit of truth about your own life. And it's killing you, you idiot. You're getting worse and worse. Do you want to hear a little about your life? Of course not! You don't want to; you're like an ostrich with its head in the sand. But you're going to listen to this. It'll show you how you've been playing out the same sick shit for decades. Let me look for it.

—I forbid you to continue!

—I was piecing together a section of your notes the other day . . . for once you were not talking about socialism or union organizing and so on. I was surprised that you had introduced your own thoughts by lifting entire paragraphs from this novel . . . it was in French but I've translated it into English. So we won't get into any misunderstanding. Here it is. . . . It's a letter one of the characters in the novel is writing to somebody. You underlined it. I'll read it quickly. ". . . I no longer want to answer you, and maybe the embarrassment I experience at this moment is itself proof that I shouldn't. However, I don't want to give you any reason to complain, I want to convince you that I've done everything I could for you. I've given you permission to write me, you say? I agree, but when you remind me, do you think that I've forgotten under what condition it was given? If I had been as faithful as you, would you have received a single response from me?"

—It all seems totally irrelevant.

—It's only the introduction to something you had to say about your son. It goes on: "Relinquish that language I cannot wish to understand; renounce that sentiment that offends me, and frightens me, and to which, maybe, you should be less attached, knowing that it's the obstacle that separates us. This sentiment, is it the only one you know?" Let me skip a few lines. "You can see my frankness, it must prove my confidence in you. It remains for you to increase it." . . . That's what you lifted intact from the text, but the following part you wrote by numbering the words. It runs on for several pages, but it only amounts to a letter. . . . "Good beginning but it's not valid in this case, in order to answer his letter. It's quite possible that my son doesn't want an answer, it's possible he won't read it, if he receives it. I write a reply and don't send it, such is my situation. I write for my own relief. If I had his letter in front of me it would be so easy, what was he saying? They didn't even give me time for a second reading; they tore the letter away from me and put it back in that big box they carry. I'm going to rewrite it. I hope not to change it. I hope I could change it. Its content is still burning in me, but the words? I'd give anything to read each word again, and look for a hint of affection. . . . 'My father! What relief it would be to know that you've read this letter, but I will only know that on the beautiful day you're set free. I must speak to you sincerely; this feeling for you is quite new. I've only understood you now that you're in prison. I must first of all explain to you that I'm back in Argentina. When I received Mother's letter I came back. She was alone, I had to take care of her. I couldn't bear to be present when you were in the house; I couldn't stand you. She was always a nervous wreck, and it was all your fault. She never knew what hour you were coming back to the house each day, but she always had to be there waiting for you. If you didn't find her there you would make the whole house shake with your shouting. She always lived in fear of your rages. I used to hate you for that, I left because of that . . . I came back hoping to find my mother in good shape, finally liberated from you, but no, on the contrary, she had gone to pieces. . . .' My son hated me;

he says that his mother hated me also, that she was afraid of me. My son tells me in his letter that my disappearance has left my wife in a bad state, that he expected, to the contrary, to find her completely renewed, relieved. But no, my wife loves me, my son he says that she cannot bear my absence, but that he is on hand to help her in every possible way. He says my wife is secluded at home, waiting for me to come out of jail at any moment. My son confesses that he couldn't stand me. He says that they weren't even able to breathe freely in the house when I was there. If I were sleeping, if I were studying, they had to be quiet. I used to go into a terrifying rage if anyone disturbed me. I no longer loved him, it's true. When he grew up I no longer loved him; he disappointed me constantly. To experience some tenderness for him I had to think how sweet and gracious he was as a baby. He left for Europe when he was a little over twenty. I had always been unhappy with him, he says that I demanded too much, that I demanded too much from everybody. From his mother, from him, from myself. I was tireless; it was always necessary for me to write, to conjoin theory and praxis, to unite the oppressed. My son wanted to be a theater director. He left. He succeeded in accomplishing nothing. Maybe I was not wrong after all; he lacked the capacity, he didn't work hard enough. He became a house painter; after that he taught Spanish in a secondary school. The triumph of my son in Paris. He married a girl who was involved in an amateur theater group. I believe she raised and lowered the curtain. That's how he entered the theater, not in a very auspicious manner. They didn't have children because life in Paris is too expensive. But he returned to his country when his mother summoned him. Then he had a change of mind. Without me his mother was more excitable than ever. I had been a matchless example of dignity in my country, I didn't get involved in petty intrigues; I didn't accept compromises; I fought to the last. In this dungeon, they even staged an execution here in a room; two men with pistols shot at me with blanks. Three times they pretended to execute me. They said the bullets were real, but their aim was off. Maybe my son would have preferred that the bullets had been real. My son and my wife are finally at peace. They have the whole house to themselves. My son tells me that he wakes up during the night and can't sleep; he feels ill; he thinks of me. I am in prison, old, sick; he's afraid for me; he feels ill; he has misjudged me all his life; how is that possible? A mistake that has lasted all his life, but now he realizes that I was truly devoted to a great cause. He regrets his mistake; he gets up during the night and can't sleep any longer and thinks of me. He feels guilty for my death because he wishes it. I understand; I was happy when he left, almost twenty years ago, because I no longer had to see him, mediocre as he was. That means I must have wanted him dead. Now all would be different, if I were able to see him. I would try to discover in him the qualities that I had not been able to see before. But it is very difficult to survive in this dark room. I am sick; I am old. Would they be happy if I died? Possibly yes. Life would continue for them, a new life. They could make noise in the house; my wife would be able to go out; she wouldn't have to stay cloistered in the house while waiting for my release from prison. She waits for me because she's afraid I may arrive and not find her there. She's afraid of me, that's why she does not go out. If I died she would finally be able to go out. The streets, even if they are jammed with Fascist patrols, would seem to her free and sunny."

—I don't believe a word of it. It's all twisted, according to your whims. I can't see what you got out of that. Changing the text.

—What was it that you wanted to say, then?

—I see very clearly that you're not qualified to do this work.

—Thanks for your support, but the text has not been altered. These are your thoughts, and you felt them so deeply that you took the trouble to encode a French text to express yourself.

—Yes, all that trouble to have an irresponsible young man come along and play with it, erase the numbers, change them, write a whole new text . . . for a motive beyond my understanding.

—I'm not your son. Or how you saw him. God knows what he was in actuality. You've always tried to treat me as if I were your son. I understand that now.

—Again those shrinks! What son are you talking about? I wanted to discover the human being in you. And I finally touched it. It's dust, dust gathered in a corner of some powerful multinational corporation building in New York, a corner in a dark basement.

—You're really going mad.

—I see you don't like to be described in detail.

—I'm stupid for getting angry at you. It's not worth it. . . . Anyhow, I hope you can find a way out, someday.

— . . .

—They were killed, your wife, your son and the poor French girl that raised curtains. Planting a bomb in your house was enough. One day you wished them dead, and the wish came true. And that drove you out of your mind, sick as you already were from the dungeon and torture. . . . But we all wish each other dead at a certain point! What do you think people are? People are like that!

—No, that's what I don't want to believe. That's the way you are, period.

—That's the way I am, and you, too. That's human essence, shit!

—I don't want to believe it.

—Accept it and live in peace.

—No, if that were true I wouldn't be able to make this

great effort to live. It's an immense effort, though not for you. That's the difference between us—you accept the shit; I don't.

—I don't like it, but it's real. What I was born into. Maybe you were luckier.

—Me? Luckier?

—Yes, Mr. Ramirez, I'm sure. Your wife waited for you until the end.

— . . .

— . . .

—Larry . . . don't believe what I said, it was . . . just to try your patience. Forgive me.

— . . .

—Come on, don't be stubborn . . . reflect and tell me . . . that you prefer to stay with me, instead of reaping all the benefits of Montreal. Because . . . because in a way you appreciate my company.

— . . .

—Think it over, calmly. . . . Leave that magazine alone!

— . . .

—Don't irritate me even more. Look me in the eyes, raise your head. . . . Don't stay there reading; just say you appreciate my friendship.

— . . .

—Put that magazine down! It isn't even yours! It's stolen from the garbage; you didn't buy it!

— . . .

— . . .

—Mr. Ramirez, the truth is I don't appreciate your friendship, why should I lie to you? You lie enough to yourself. I made this sacrifice until now because I needed the money. But you are unbearable; one never knows what stupidity you will come out with. Suddenly you turn against people, and I don't understand why.

—Say more, say that I'm unpredictable, that you never

know when I'm going to explode in a cold rage. And don't forget the most important thing, say that I disappointed you.

—You did. Maybe all old people disappoint their juniors. I never felt well in your company.

— . . .

— . . .

—Is there a university near Palm Springs?

—I don't know. Why?

—I'll be able to find somebody capable enough to work on my books there. Don't worry about the hours you have already devoted to this. All you have to do is give me an estimate, and I'll see that you're paid. I don't know the rate; maybe it should be the same as for your wheeling me around, including conversation. I mean the second rate we agreed upon.

— . . .

—I think I should pay your fares, the subway fares for your trips to Columbia, and telephone calls. I know it's just a few cents, but I don't want to take advantage of anyone, even if the sum is petty.

—That's very kind of you, but it's not necessary. I am prepared to continue the work on my own without the financial support of the University of Montreal, if it comes to that.

—There is no work to be continued. I'm taking my books with me.

—What's there to say? Now you no longer have any influence over me. Who will listen to you? And be your friend?

—There's nothing to say. I no longer want to have any influence on you, and you were never my friend.

— . . .

—You can be nobody's friend.

—I'm going.

—I gave you lots of things, though my means are modest;

but you never gave me anything, not even one of your precious magazines from the garbage can, not even a piece of candy . . .

— . . .

— . . . that I craved so much. Those who can't give anything, can't give for some reason. That's all, I guess . . . send me the bill by mail. I wouldn't like to see you again.

— . . .

—But you're the winner, Larry, although you may not realize it. You finally convinced me.

— . . .

—I'm glad your mother threw you out, and that your wife left you, and that nobody would come to a class of yours anywhere. As much as I suffered when I heard those sad troubles of yours, now satisfaction overwhelms me. I've been able to feel that old joy again! Lowness, revenge, resentment: to me they were empty words, but not anymore. Now I feel them and understand them very well. You won, Larry, you've convinced me. I'm also the thing you name so often and with such relish. I enjoy your misfortune.

— . . .

— . . .

—Bye.
—Bye.

—Mr. Ramirez . . .

—Get out . . .

—Mr. Ramirez . . . help me . . .

—Where are you? . . . I can't see you . . .

—I'm far away; I'm in danger.

—I'll have nothing to do with you.

—Mr. Ramirez . . . have mercy . . .

—Just tell me where you are.

—I don't know . . . I don't dare look around me.

—Don't be a coward. If you describe the landscape . . .
I'll try to figure it out. What is it about . . . this time?

—Thank you . . .

— . . .

—Mr. Ramirez . . . I can see . . . two small rooms . . .

—They are small, but cozy.

—Two small rooms. The stove is in one, and is covered
with grease, stalactites of grease and dust. Everything sticks
to it. And there's no furniture, only a broken chair I found
in the street. And on the floor, newspaper shreds that drifted
in from God knows where. There's a mattress on the floor
and a sheet that used to be white, but has turned brown. And
roaches galore.

—And the blanket? Haven't you got a blanket?

—No, I'm never cold. Sometimes I have to turn off the
heat. And I sleep without a pillow; it's healthier like that.
You can see the filth in the apartment from the street or the
neighbor's window.

—Somebody is looking at you from the street, it's the man
you're afraid of.

—Yes, it's him . . .

—Why? Does he know you?

—He's very silent and doesn't complain. Then suddenly
he explodes.

—Why? Who is he? How hard would he hit you?

—Very hard.

—I'm sure you deserve it. So once and for all leave me in peace; I've told you I don't want anything to do with you.

—You're to blame for all this.

—Get out . . . I've had enough . . . enough! Do you hear me?

—You're to blame because you told me to put myself in his hands.

—What for?

—To give him the choice. Once in his hands he could do anything he wanted to me.

—I don't trust that man, Larry, he could destroy you, annihilate you.

—But if you knew that, why did you tell me to put myself in his hands?

—I don't know. I've forgotten why.

—Maybe you want to see me dead, that's why.

—Maybe.

—What have I done to you to deserve this?

—I don't remember what you've done to me. Could you've forgotten about the limits of my memory? As for you, all I know is that I'll never be able to forgive you.

—Mr. Ramirez . . . he's staring at me, through the window. He can see me because there are no curtains.

—Sometimes he doesn't know what he's doing.

—Yes, Mr. Ramirez, he's nervous, he loses control . . .

—It's not that he's nervous, he's sullen, and tolerant . . . then he explodes, you can never tell when . . .

—You got me into this, now you must help me!

—Close the door, don't let him in . . .

—It's too late. He's in this room, he's disgusted by the sight of the greasy stove. The roaches flee in panic.

—Jump out the window, try to dodge him, do something.

—It's too late. I saw him passing by in the street. His face had turned white, he was cold with rage.

—What do you think he's going to do to you now?

—He's going to wring my neck, snap my head off, smash my head in, like kids do to their dolls. He'll break my limbs.

—Will you survive?

—Maybe, but as a bloody messed-up sight.

—Larry . . . please . . . don't say any more . . .

— . . .

—Larry . . . don't say any more of those horrible things . . . but show me some sign of life . . .

— . . .

—Larry! . . . Answer me!

—You can take a doll's head in your hand, crush in its forehead and temples. Then you can put one hand around its chest, the other around its head, and twist its body one way and its head the other It's like wringing a towel, snapping its head off. Snap its arms off like twigs. Your hands are big enough to fit around the doll. Split its legs apart . . . the way you split open a chicken, ripping the cartilage, tearing the flesh, then chewing the meat.

—Larry . . . ask him to forgive you . . . do something . . .

—Everything is useless . . . there's nothing left to do. . . . He's just told me that he'll never forgive me.

—Larry . . .

— . . .

—Larry! Show me a sign of life!

— . . .

—Larry! . . .

— . . .

Palm Springs Nursing Home
456 Sunny Road
Palm Springs, CA 43098

January 30, 1978

Dear Mr. Margulies,

I've been trying to reach you unsuccessfully by telephone for over a week, to obtain your permission to transfer Mr. Juan José Ramirez to a psychiatric hospital in Los Angeles. I wanted to know whether you had any recommendations as to hospitals, since their rates vary. There was no alternative to transferring Mr. Ramirez to a place where he could receive psychiatric care, since his condition was rapidly deteriorating. He was extremely depressed, ate less and less, and could not be coaxed out of his bed even for short outings in his wheelchair.

His blood pressure dropped considerably late Friday afternoon. Since I knew I could not reach you over the weekend I took the liberty of having him transferred by ambulance to the Good Samaritan Hospital in Los Angeles. The vehicle left at 6 P.M. and at 8:30 P.M. I received a call from Dr. Edith Manska saying that the patient had arrived.

Trusting you will understand the actions we have taken, I am respectfully yours,

Dr. Conrad Schroeder
Director

Human Rights International
Reception Committee
43 Gramercy Park
New York, NY 10027

February 4, 1978

Dear Mr. Ramirez,

I hope these few lines will find you well on your way to recovery. I was out of town for a week, and on returning found Dr. Schroeder's letter with the news of your transfer to the Good Samaritan Hospital in Los Angeles. At first I was quite disappointed, since I felt sure that all the expense and inconvenience of your transfer to Palm Springs would be worthwhile. After having thought it over, I consider what has happened inevitable. You must be physically exhausted after being forced to adjust to so many different places in such a short period of time. I suggest that you stay at the Good Samaritan for as long as you feel it's necessary. Concerning an eventual return to Palm Springs, which I endorse strongly, please let us know your opinions on the matter.

I'm enclosing this unsealed envelope that was forwarded to me by Saint Vincent's Hospital in New York City. I didn't send it sooner because it arrived at my office during my absence. Apparently it was found under the mattress of your bed right after you had left the hospital to be taken to the airport. Also, it took them a while to forward it to us. Since the envelope reads "To whom it may concern," I opened it. Knowing the contents, I am wondering whether you want us to keep it for you. In that case, please send it back to me with all the instructions you think necessary.

In any event, I hope to hear from you soon, hopefully

with good news. With best wishes for a speedy recovery, yours truly,

Eli Margulies
Secretary of Internal Affairs

Saint Vincent's Hospital
New York

Christmas Night 77

This is my last will and testament. I am very pleased to state that I have a nice present to leave behind. All that I possess are these four books, with some numbers penciled in them. But they can be of use to a person I deeply appreciate, my friend Larry, the attendant hired by the committee.

This has been a very nice day; and now I'm convinced that things will definitely improve for me in the future.

Juan José Ramirez

Los Angeles Hospital, Psychiatric Ward

February 4, 1978

Dear Mr. Margulies:

We regret to announce the death of Mr. Juan José Ramirez, which took place two days ago, on the morning of the 2nd of February.

His condition had not improved since his arrival. He received psychiatric treatment daily, but none of the symptoms subsided. Our impression is that his poor physical condition could not cope with the deep depression he was experiencing, caused by his long confinement in his native country. His blood pressure dropped once again that morning and there was no way to reverse his decline.

There was no special request from the patient during his last hours of life. He said he would be relieved to end his suffering, and had nothing to leave behind, except a few books that he was donating to our library. Asked whether he preferred to be buried in some particular place or cremated, he said that we should use the most economical method, since the funds of the committee over which you preside should be used for the living and not the dead.

We await your instructions as to how to proceed.

Sincerely yours,

Dr. Alfred Piñones
Director, Psychiatric Ward

Lawrence John
41 Carmine St.
New York, NY 10014

February 17, 1978

Dear Mr. Margulies:

I have received your letter of February 15th asking me for a written statement about the contradictory requests of Mr. Juan José Ramirez for the disposition of his books.

As you know, I have been recently working on these texts, decoding the notes that he made while he was in prison. I have been in contact with the Universities of Columbia and Montreal, which are very interested in supporting my research and seeing that it reaches the light of day. I should like to continue this work, which will demonstrate Mr. Ramirez' achievements, rather than have the books collect dust in a hospital library. I'm convinced that his prison notes are of significant historical and social value. He devoted the best years of his life to the struggle for political ideals and surely would have wanted that struggle to continue after his death. He had agreed to have me work on the notes and publish the results as part of a project sponsored by the Institute for Latin American Studies of the University of Montreal.

On the last day that I attended him his condition had deteriorated badly; he was no longer able to reason and keep his mind on the present. He felt threatened by everybody and everything, and accused me of being his enemy. We had an argument, after which he wanted to break off all relations with me. His change of opinion in this regressed state should not be allowed to override his former desires.

Respectfully yours,

Lawrence John

Human Rights International
Reception Committee
43 Gramercy Park
New York, NY 10027

February 22, 1978

Dear Mr. John,

Thank you for your kind letter of the 17th. I see that you understand the difficulties of my position in regards to this case. I was inclined to accept the solution you proposed, since there was no conclusive evidence of Mr. Ramirez' opposition to your participation in the project. Unfortunately, other evidence has come to my attention that I cannot possibly ignore. Soon after writing to you I received a telephone call from an employee at the Greenwich Village Home, where Mr. Ramirez had been residing for some time. It was from a Mrs. Ann Lewis, a nurse who requested information about the demise of Mr. Ramirez. Mrs. Lewis had received the sad news of Mr. Ramirez' death and was both shocked and sorry to hear that the end had come so quickly. She wanted to know more about the patient's last days, and during our conversation I discovered that she had last spoken with Mr. Ramirez minutes before he was taken from Saint Vincent's Hospital to the airport to be flown to California. He had called her to say good-bye, because, according to Mrs. Lewis, she was the only person he had got along with at the Village Home. She found him very depressed. She also stated that Mr. Ramirez complained strongly about you and cautioned her against having any dealings with you. According to Mr. Ramirez your conduct had been rather unacceptable.

Given the nature of the case, I was obliged to ask Mrs. Lewis if she had found the patient greatly altered. She assured me that this was not the case, that although he sounded very sad, he was composed and lucid. At that point I thought it necessary to inform Mrs. Lewis of the problem concerning the two contradictory letters. She then repeated what Mr. Ramirez had told her. According to him, you had contrived to exclude Mr. Ramirez from the project at the University of Montreal, and he no longer wished to have any association with you.

I'm sure you will understand that the existence of this witness makes it impossible for me to consider any participation on your part in potential projects based upon Mr. Ramirez' books. Surely something will come of this material, but not necessarily at the University of Montreal, with which we have had no relations in the past. We are, however, grateful to you for pointing out the value of these documents, and there is no doubt that steps will be taken for the publication of the works. Our organization is deeply interested in the study of such subjects.

I hope you'll understand how difficult it was for me to arrive at this inevitable conclusion. Please accept my apologies for not having been able to clarify the situation at an earlier date.

Sincerely yours,

Eli Margulies
Secretary of Internal Affairs

New York State Employment Agency
25 Church Street
New York, NY 10013

JOB APPLICATION
Name: Lawrence John
Nationality: USA
Date of birth: February 27, 1942
Marital Status: Divorced
Education: Ph.D. in History, New York University, graduated 1970
Previous Employment: Professor of History at Saint Anthony of Padua's College, Brooklyn, June 1971 to December 1973
Bartender, The Mikado restaurant, MacDougall St., 1974
Gardener, the estate of Mr. James Austin, East Hampton, Long Island, 1974 to 1976
Waiter, Salerno restaurant, Broome St., 1977
Attendant at Greenwich Village Home, 1977 to 1978
Employment desired: any

Attention: Mr. Brown, Professional Employment Department

Dear Mr. Brown: Excuse me for writing you this way, on the back of the application form, but I had nothing else to write on. Maybe you remember me, I was taken to your office two years ago, in 1976, because I had refused to take a job as a college instructor, which was against welfare rules. I mean I couldn't keep collecting unemployment after refusing a job in my specialty. My pretense was to wait until another assistant-gardener position came up. I have a lot of white hair, do you remember me? Well, after all these years —six!—I've just written again "Employment desired: any" on your application form, meaning anything as long as it is modest. But right now I have a peculiar idea and I'm going to cross out that last line.

I've changed my mind and I'm willing to take a college job of responsibility. But not any job, not teaching, for instance. I want something with direct contact with research programs; I wouldn't like to repeat a mistake I once made. Something in sociopolitical research would be ideal. Even better, something having to do with unions. Don't unions ever ask for the assistance of sociologists? Of course, it shouldn't be just any union; it should be progressive. If worst comes to worst, it could even be reactionary; it would be useful to see how they operate from a close angle. I don't think it could contaminate me; it's not infectious like the flu. And there's always the possibility of engaging in sabotage. I'm joking. The important point is that I truly promise you to give the best that I'm capable of. Suddenly I realized that you were right. I owe this to your good advice.

I know I'm asking for something difficult, but I have a feeling that it could be arranged. On my side, there are no problems, as before, and that's already saying something. No doubt the opportunity I'm looking for will take awhile to present itself; meantime I'm willing to take any modest job. But only on a provisory basis. I apologize for my informality. I'm not under the influence of anything. I hate stimulants, I don't even drink coffee.

Who knows where I get this feeling from, that things are going to be O.K. for me now, and in unions, of all places. I feel optimistic for the first time in a long time. It must be the good seed of your advice that has sprouted at last.

I'm waiting for your call then. Many thanks in advance,

Lawrence John

MANUEL PUIG (1932–1990) was born in a small town in the Argentine pampas. Before becoming a writer, he studied philosophy at the University of Buenos Aires and worked in the film industry in Rome. Best known for his novel *Kiss of the Spider Woman*, which has been adapted as a film and a Broadway musical, Puig also wrote *Betrayed by Rita Hayworth*, *Heartbreak Tango*, and *Blood of Requited Love*, also published by the University of Minnesota Press.